Vale's job is to kill people, so when his last two targets get reanimated after he killed them, he takes it personally.

Cyril's job is to reanimate people. His ability as a necromancer means he lives a lonely life, but he's used to it. He's not looking for a relationship, and he's certainly not looking for a confrontation with a professional assassin.

Vale isn't the only person interested in talking to Cyril. When Vale finds goons from a local crime family intimidating the necromancer, he steps in, only for Cyril to freak out when he asks him why he keeps reanimating his targets.

Cyril needs protection, no matter how much he insists he doesn't. It's not Vale's job to provide it, but he finds himself wanting to shield Cyril from the people who want to force him into something he's not willing to do.

He just wishes that Cyril's weird skeleton octopus pet didn't like him so much.

First Meet With Death
Copyright © 2024 Catherine Lievens
ISBN: 978-1-4874-4173-9
Cover art by Angela Waters

Published by eXtasy Books Inc

Look for us online at:
www.eXtasybooks.com

First Meet With Death
Not Quite Dead 1

By

Catherine Lievens

CHAPTER ONE

Vale watched the man he was about to kill.

He looked pretty normal. He had neatly cut brown hair and was wearing a suit, like a lot of normal people. Vale didn't know why he was killing the guy, and he didn't care. This was what he was paid to do, just like he'd been paid to kill so many others before.

The man walked into what Vale would call a seedy motel. The sign out front was only lit on the right, and the paint was peeling from the wall by the door. There would only be a few reasons the guy was here, and Vale was ready to bet money it was to cheat on his wife. Either that or drugs, but there was no way a man like this didn't have a wife at home and probably a couple of kids, too.

Vale didn't care that the man was probably cheating on his wife. He was making things easy for Vale, which didn't always happen. Vale smiled and called Artemis.

"Already done, Roux?" she asked when she answered.

"He's getting a room. Can you find the number?"

He could hear her fingers flying over her keyboard as he gave the name of the motel and where they were. She knew what he was up to. She was his handler, which meant she'd talked to the person who'd hired him to kill the guy he was following. Vale trusted her, which was why he hadn't asked her why. She knew his limits, and she'd never broken them.

"Two-oh-five," she eventually said.

"Thank you."

"Let me know when you're done."

1

"Always."

Now that he had a room number, he waited for a few more minutes and walked into the motel as if he knew where he was going. They were all similar, anyway. He went straight for the stairs, and no one tried to stop him. The man behind the counter was too busy playing what sounded like porn on his phone, while the two guys in the corner were probably doing something illegal, from the way they kept glancing around. They weren't being discreet.

The low ceiling had stains that Vale didn't want to examine too closely. The carpet on the stairs was threadbare, and the air smelled of dust, mildew, and cigarette smoke. Vale wasn't a delicate flower, but he still wrinkled his nose and wondered if he could catch something just by breathing the air. He'd been in much worse places, but that didn't mean he enjoyed it.

Vale climbed the stairs two by two until he reached the second floor. He didn't have to go far to find room 205. It was only a few doors down, and before knocking, he took out his gun, complete with a silencer. He held it loosely and knocked. He heard creaking behind the door and readied himself.

It took the man a moment to answer. When he did, he frowned, probably because he didn't recognize Vale.

"Who are you?" he asked.

His suit jacket was gone, and he'd rolled the sleeves of his shirt up to his elbows. He'd also taken off his shoes and socks, and in the few seconds Vale had left, he cringed at the thought. Didn't the man know how dirty motel carpets were? And these were visibly stained, for fuck's sake.

Vale didn't answer the man's question. He raised his gun and fired it, putting a hole between the man's eyes. The man's shocked expression stayed on his face as he fell back.

Vale quickly put his gun away before stepping into the room. He grabbed the man's arms and dragged him deeper inside, leaving him just inside the room. He closed the door behind himself. It would take a while for anyone to find his target, and by then, Vale would be far away.

He left the motel as easily as he'd walked in. He hummed as he walked down the street toward his car, smiling at the thought of the money that would soon hit his account. He waited until he was inside the vehicle to call Artemis back.

"All done," he told her.

"Great. What will you do now?"

"I'm headed home."

"I'll make sure the money is all there by the time you land."

She would. She always did, and they'd been working together long enough that Vale trusted her with his life — and with his money.

She knew he was putting away as much as possible so he could retire. He didn't have anything against the life he lived, but he was getting older. He wasn't quite old yet, although some days, he felt like he was. He supposed that for some people, thirty-nine years old *was* old, and for others, it wasn't. His body certainly reflected the way he'd lived his life until now, and he wanted to stop working before the job became harder to deal with.

Today's job was one more step toward retirement. It would take him several more, but he was almost there, and he could already imagine his life.

With a smile on his lips, he drove away from the motel and toward the airport. It was time to go home, relax for a bit, and get ready for the next job.

As far as Cyril was concerned, there was nothing better on a rainy day than reading in his stuffy armchair while drinking tea. The only reason he wasn't bundled up in a blanket was that it was July and too warm for that, but if it had been winter, he would've had on thick socks and a blanket, and he would have made himself a nest. Reading during the summer was good, too, though. Reading was always good.

He stretched out and bumped his foot against Oscar, who was on the footrest. Oscar lazily opened one eye and whacked Cyril's foot with a tentacle. Cyril poked him with his bare toes, then let him be. At least while Oscar was sleeping, he wasn't getting into trouble.

Cyril's phone rang on the coffee table. He sighed, already knowing that his day of reading was over. Was it too much to ask to allow him to relax for once? Apparently, it was.

He grabbed his phone, along with the notepad and pen he always kept with him, and answered. "Cyril Moreau, what can I do for you?"

The woman on the other side of the phone sucked in a breath. Cyril gave her time. He already knew she'd lost someone recently, and it wasn't every day that someone called a necromancer.

"Are you a necromancer?" she asked.

"I am."

"It's my husband. He was—he was found today, dead. He was shot." She swallowed heavily. "In the head. I don't know if you can work with that."

"I sure can. He'll always have the wound, but there are ways to deal with it."

"Oh. I thought you could heal it."

"I'm not a healer, so no. I can only bring him back, and even then, there are certain conditions."

"I can pay whatever you ask for."

Cyril's heart hurt for her. He'd never lost anyone that he could remember. His father had died when he was a baby, and he only had his mother, who was still very much alive and planning to continue being so for decades to come. "It's not a question of money. Why don't you give me your name to start?"

"Liliana. Liliana Beauford."

"It's a pleasure to make your acquaintance. Can you tell me more about what happened and about your husband? What's his name?"

"Francis. He's, well, he was found shot in the head."

"When did it happen?"

"Earlier today."

So the death was very recent. That would be helpful. "That's a good thing. The sooner I can reach a body after they die, the easier the reanimation is. What were you thinking about? Do you want it to be temporary?"

That was the bulk of Cyril's job. Sometimes people died without telling their loved ones where they'd left family heirlooms or who they wanted their inheritance to go to. He'd also worked for the police force when they needed to know what happened to someone. No one had called him for this death, so it probably meant they wouldn't. They were wary of him on the best of days and outright hated him on the worst. Besides, it wasn't like anything the victims would say would be admissible in court. For some reason, people thought that Cyril might be able to convince the dead bodies he reanimated to say things. They didn't understand how it worked, and while it was ridiculous, Cyril couldn't exactly blame them for that. Necromancy was a mysterious art for the people who weren't necromancers, and even more so, it was scary.

"No." Mrs. Beauford's voice trembled. "Can you reanimate him permanently?"

"I can certainly do that. He died recently enough, but I have to warn you that he might be different. He was shot in the head, and those are always the trickiest wounds and the trickiest deaths to reanimate."

"That's fine." She sobbed just once before making a

muffled sound as if she were pressing a tissue against her lips. "I just want him back. Our kids deserve to have a father."

Cyril grimaced, but he didn't try to change her mind. He'd tried that in the past when he could see that the person he'd been called to reanimate wouldn't be the same person their family had known before. That was especially true when it came to head wounds. He couldn't heal wounds. He could only reanimate the dead, and when he did, they were in the same state as they had been after dying, except that they weren't dead anymore. If Mrs. Beauford wanted her husband to be like he'd been before, she would have to find a good healer, and there weren't many around.

Thankfully, Cyril had friends and people that he regularly worked with. "I can give you the names of a few healers I work with. They should be able to help you once your husband is reanimated."

"Really? I don't know how to thank you."

"You don't have to." After all, Cyril wasn't doing this out of the goodness of his heart. He was doing it because he'd be paid handsomely for it. Any permanent reanimation was very costly because of the amount of power he had to put into it. "Why don't you tell me where I'm supposed to go?"

He wrote down all the details he could remember from the conversation and the address where she'd be waiting for him. He wasn't surprised to recognize it. Her husband had been brought to the morgue. When he went, he'd probably encounter a detective working on the man's death. He might be lucky and not have to deal with Detective Anderson, but what would be the odds? Detective Anderson always seemed to catch the deaths Cyril was called to reanimate.

"When can you be here? I'd like to take my husband home tonight," Mrs. Beauford said.

Cyril looked at the sky outside his window. It was still raining, but while he wished he could stay home and continue reading his book, time was of the essence when it came to re-animations. "I can be there in an hour if that's all right with you."

Mrs. Beauford sobbed again. "That would be perfect."

Once they'd hung up, Cyril stretched. Oscar was still lounging on the footrest, and Cyril let him sleep. He wouldn't be taking him on this job. He didn't want to shock Mrs. Beauford, and generally, people didn't react well to seeing Oscar. They thought he was weird—and Cyril could admit he was—but it didn't mean he was dangerous or evil.

Cyril quickly dressed and headed out. He wrinkled his nose at the water coming down from the sky, then climbed into his car and headed to the morgue. He knew the drive so well that he could probably have driven his car with his eyes closed. Most of the reanimations he worked on happened at the morgue.

Once he got there, he grabbed his bag and went inside. He smiled at Janet, who was at the front desk today. She smiled back, but it wasn't very warm. Like everyone, she was wary of Cyril, even though she knew him and saw him at least once a week.

"Who?" she asked.

"Francis Beauford."

Janet grimaced. "Detective Anderson won't be happy."

Cyril groaned. "I won't be happy, either. I like dealing with him as much as he enjoys dealing with me."

Janet snickered. "That sounds about right."

Cyril was very much aware of the tension between him and Detective Anderson, and he didn't need Janet to remind him. He waved at her and walked down the hallway, ready to face Detective Anderson. He didn't even have to walk into the room where the body was kept to encounter him. Detective Anderson was in the hallway, talking to a woman wearing a dark green dress. Her blonde hair was piled up on top of her head, and she looked like she'd been crying. She was shaking her head at something Detective Anderson was saying.

"You don't have to autopsy him to know how he died," she said. "It's obvious."

"I know he was shot, Mrs. Beauford, but there could be something we're missing, something we'd find only during an autopsy. We don't know why he was at that motel, for example."

The woman's expression hardened. "I've already called a necromancer."

Detective Anderson's back went ramrod straight. He was a big man with dark blond hair cut short. He was wearing a suit, and Cyril already knew he also had a tie on. He was always very neat, even when he visited the morgue.

"Who?" Detective Anderson asked.

Cyril cleared his throat. "Mrs. Beauford?"

The woman looked at him. "Are you the necromancer?"

"I am."

Detective Anderson turned to look at Cyril. He was glaring so hard that Cyril wouldn't be surprised to end up dead on one of the metal tables nearby. He was only doing what he was being paid to do, but that wouldn't stop Detective Anderson from holding him personally responsible.

"I should have known it was you," Detective Anderson said with a snarl.

Cyril kept a smile on his face. "I *am* the best in the city." He turned his attention back to Mrs. Beauford. "I'm ready when you are. Shall we go inside and take a look at your husband?"

She gave him a watery smile and nodded. When Cyril started to walk past Detective Anderson to follow Mrs. Beauford inside, Detective Anderson caught his arm.

"You shouldn't be allowed to do this. She didn't agree to an autopsy because of you. We'll lose precious evidence."

Cyril pulled his arm away. "I don't have anything to do

with that. She asked me if I could do this, and I can."

"How much is she paying you?"

"That's none of your business. It's the law, Detective Anderson. I had nothing to do with how it was created or why." Since dead people could be reanimated, there was a law in place that allowed the deceased's family to deny an autopsy. They wouldn't want one to have been performed if they were paying for their loved one to be reanimated.

It was the reason a lot of the cops Cyril came into contact with disliked him, almost as if he'd been the one to create the law. He hadn't been. He didn't have anything to do with it, although he could admit it made his life easier.

The rest of the cops disliked him because they thought he was weird and were afraid of him. That was something he was used to, too.

Detective Anderson made a frustrated noise and stepped aside. Cyril didn't look back as he followed Mrs. Beauford. This wasn't the first time he'd had to deal with Detective Anderson's foul mood, and it wouldn't be the last.

Lucky him.

Chapter Two

By the time Vale got home, almost twenty-four hours had passed. His first plane had been late, which meant he'd missed his connection. He'd had to wait hours in the airport, and he was exhausted, even though he'd done nothing more than sitting around and wasting time on his phone.

He unlocked his front door, stepped inside, and dropped his bag. He was tempted to go straight to bed, but he needed a shower first. He wanted to wash the airplane and airports off his skin.

His phone rang as he headed toward the bathroom. He took it out and answered without looking who it was since only a few people had his number. It could be either his best friend or Artemis—Rachel, when they weren't working.

"Hello?" he answered.

"There's a problem," Artemis said.

Vale groaned and closed his eyes. "I wasn't paid for the hit?" That was the only thing he could think of.

"The client is refusing to pay because the dead guy is still alive."

Vale blinked. "I'm sorry?"

"You heard me. Your target is still alive."

"That's not possible. I shot him in the head. No one survives that kind of shot."

"I know that, and I believe you, but the client doesn't. He's pissed that the target is still walking around, and he's refusing to pay. He said he was going to hire someone else."

"He's certainly free to do that, but I did my job." Vale

swore because he'd counted on that money. *Dammit.*

He eyed his bed. He'd left it neatly made, and after spending the past week away from it, the only thing he wanted to do was to shower and dive right in between the sheets. His eyes burned from the lack of sleep, and he was also slightly hangry.

"He could be trying to get out of paying me," Vale said as he started moving again.

"I thought about that, but when I checked, the target was alive. I found recent footage of him."

She was a wizard when it came to hacking into security cameras all over the country, and she was one of Vale's best friends. She would never lie to him. That meant the target was alive, even though Vale had shot him in the head.

He put his phone down on the bathroom counter and pressed the speaker button. Artemis's voice came out loud and clear as Vale took off his t-shirt.

"What do you want me to do?" she asked.

"I don't think there's much we can do. I did my job, but the target is still alive, and the client won't pay. It's not like I can go after him." Although it was tempting. Vale had done what he'd been paid to do. It would only be right for him to get the money, and he disliked that the client was throwing a hissy fit.

"I'm really sorry."

Vale sighed. "Not your fault. I'm sure you tried everything you thought of to convince him to stop being an asshole."

"I did. I can find you another job. You can make up for the money you just lost."

Vale chewed on his lower lip as he thought. He didn't *need* another job now, and he was curious.

He'd killed that guy. He was sure of it. He knew some people could reanimate dead bodies, but he'd never encountered that kind of situation in all the years he'd been practicing. He was curious to find out what had happened, because reanimations weren't cheap.

"Can you book me a ticket back?" he asked as he shed his jeans.

"Of course. Why are you heading back, though?"

"I want to check out what happened. I'm curious."

"I get that, but do you really think it's a good idea?"

"I don't think it's a *bad* idea. I won't try to find the client to beat the shit out of him, so don't worry about that. It's not worth my time."

She snickered. "You're right. I'll book you a plane ticket and continue looking into it. If you did your job, it's only right that the client pays, whatever happens after you're done. If he still doesn't want to after I have proof you did what you were paid to do, I'll just take the money from him and ensure he's banned from the job board."

"See? This is why I love you. I need you to take care of me."

"Always."

"I miss seeing your face."

Vale saw Russell much more often than they saw Rachel. She was on the move a lot, like Vale and Russell, but since she was their handler, she didn't need to meet them to work with them. At least once a year, the three of them managed to be in the same city and see each other, but that was it. Vale hoped that once he retired, it would be easier for the three of them to find a way to make it work, and he was almost there, but not quite.

"I miss seeing your face, too. It's been too long." There was wishfulness in Rachel's voice.

"We should organize something."

"I'm on it," Rachel promised. She was Rachel now because they weren't talking about work anymore. "I already booked you a plane ticket. You leave tomorrow."

That would give Vale time to rest for a bit and take care of a few things. "Thank you."

"Nothing to thank me for. You know I always have your back, and so does Russell."

"Yeah."

"Keep me updated."

Vale would, just like he'd call Russell after he was done with his shower and had a few hours of sleep. His best friend would find this situation hilarious, and now that Vale knew he'd get the money in some way, he felt the same. He'd killed the target, and the target was back. That didn't happen every day.

He hoped it would never happen to him again.

Cyril groaned when his phone rang. He needed some rest after the reanimation he'd done for Mrs. Beauford, but the people who called him didn't always understand that. Some of them got angry when he told them he couldn't work for them and sent them the way of one of his competitors. He was the best in the city, which meant a lot of wealthy clients flocked to him. They were never happy when he told them to fuck off—albeit in better terms.

He had to sit up to grab his phone, which meant dislodging Oscar from his chest. Oscar opened one eye and glared at Cyril, but Cyril ignored him, knowing his pet would settle down again once he stopped moving.

Cyril smiled when he saw that the caller wasn't a client but his mother. He quickly answered because he *did* want to talk to his mom.

"I thought for sure you wouldn't answer," she said as Cyril settled back down on the couch.

Oscar crawled higher on his chest and flopped down, tickling one tentacle along Cyril's neck. Cyril batted it away. "Why wouldn't I answer your calls?"

"Well, you might be working or dead in a ditch some-where."

Cyril snorted. "None of my clients has ever killed me."

"For now, but remember that you didn't get your ability from my side of the family."

Cyril grinned. His mother wasn't happy with his job, not because she thought it was weird or unnatural but because she was protective of him. His father had died on a job when Cyril was a baby, so he understood where his mother was coming from. His father had refused to reanimate someone, and that person's family hadn't taken it well. Cyril didn't know any details, and his mother had always told him that it didn't matter because it had been almost thirty years.

Maybe she was right. Did it really matter how Cyril's father had died? Cyril had grown up without his father, without an-yone who could teach him how to be a necromancer. He had an innate ability, but that didn't mean he'd known what to do right from the start. His mother was a good woman, and she'd raised him even after she realized he had the same ability as his father, but it hadn't been easy for either of them.

"I'm sure you'd hire someone to reanimate me just so you could yell at me for getting myself killed," he teased.

"Damn right, I would. I didn't work so hard to get you to adulthood only to have you killed. What are you up to today? Working?"

"No. I did a permanent reanimation the other day, so I'm taking it slow today."

"You do too many of those."

"Possibly, but they pay well, and I never say no to money."

Cyril's mother grumbled, but they both remembered how hard the first years without his father had been. Cyril never wanted his mother to have to work two or three jobs again. He had an incredible ability that very few people had, and he intended to use it to make his and his mother's lives easier and happier.

"You need to be careful, baby," his mother said.

"I always am. You don't have to worry about me."

"You're my only child. When am I not going to worry about you? I started worrying when you reanimated that fly when you were two, and I never stopped."

Cyril had been a precocious child. He didn't remember any of that, of course, but his mother often told him about how he'd found a dead fly in his crib. She'd leaned down to pick it up and throw it away, but before she could, Cyril had grabbed it. His mother had thought for sure he would stuff it into his mouth, but instead, he'd opened his palm, and she'd seen the fly coming back to life. She'd known then that he was like his father, and she'd done everything she could to help him deal with his ability. It was thanks to her that he'd found someone to tutor him and ensure he didn't make mistakes. She'd always been there for him, and now, it was time for him to be there for her.

"I promise I'll be fine," he murmured.

"At the very least, you'll be careful."

"I will."

He wished he could do more to make her feel better, but this was his life. There was no running from it or ignoring it. He'd been born with this ability, and there was no getting rid of it. He'd learned to make the most out of what he had, and he would continue doing so.

CHAPTER THREE

Vale was back, and he wasn't happy about it. Unfortunately for him, if he wanted to find out what had happened to his last target, this was where he needed to be. He grumbled as he parked his rented car in the hotel parking lot and got out. Once again, he'd traveled light, so he only had one bag. He hauled it over his shoulder as he made his way toward the hotel entrance, but his phone vibrating in his pocket gave him pause.

He slid it out and smiled at Artemis's name on the screen. "I barely even landed, and you're already calling me?" he answered.

"I thought you might be interested in another job in town."

Vale wanted to say no. He was here to satisfy his curiosity, but he'd go home soon. On the other hand, he was already here. He might as well put his time to good use. "Yeah, I'll take it," he said as he made his way to the front desk.

He slid his ID—a fake one—onto the desk toward the woman behind it. She took it with a smile and went to work, checking him in. He'd be more careful this time and snap pictures once he was done, but this was his bread and butter, and he didn't see a problem with doing this job while he was here.

"Give me a few days to go over everything, and it'll be done," he told Artemis as the concierge took his credit card.

"I'll put your name down for it, then."

"You do that, and please send me all the information you have. I'll go over it once I'm settled in my hotel room."

They said their goodbyes, and Vale hung up. He hadn't

come here thinking he'd do a job, but he was always armed, so it wouldn't be a problem. Besides, if he needed something different from what he carried, he knew where to go.

The concierge gave Vale everything back, along with his room key. He nodded at her in thanks, relieved to be already done with the annoying part of this trip. Now that he had a room, he could wash off the plane and head out to discover what the fuck had happened to his previous target.

He made his way upstairs, quickly opening the email with the information Artemis had sent his way. Just like he'd expected, it would be an easy job. He had a name, a list of places where his target could be found, and a decent amount of money that would be transferred into his account once the job was done.

His phone rang again before he could get even close to the bathroom. He groaned and almost decided to ignore it, but again, it could only be a handful of people, and all of them would be worried if he didn't answer. When he picked up his phone from the desk where he'd left it, he knew he was right. Russell would have hounded him until he picked up the phone, which meant he wouldn't have been able to shower in peace.

"Why are you calling me?" Vale asked.

"Your last target got up and walked away?" Russell teased with laughter in his tone.

Even though Russell couldn't see him, Vale rolled his eyes. This was the reaction of pretty much anyone who spent any length of time with Russell. He might be a great shot and professional when he was working, but he was also annoying as fuck.

"He didn't walk away, at least not while I was there."

Russell guffawed. "But he did eventually. Rachel told me what happened."

"Did she also tell you that the client was refusing to pay

me?"

"I'm not surprised. I'm not saying it's right, but put your-self in their shoes. They paid you to kill a guy, and he's still alive."

"I wouldn't say he's still alive. He's alive again."

"How is that any different?"

"In the way that I killed him. He was dead and had a bullet in his head. No one could survive that, and I'm sure he didn't."

"Reanimation?"

"Yeah, I think so. That's what Rachel believes, anyway."

"She told me that, too. She also said that's why you went back. Do you really think it's a good idea to poke at a necro-mancer?"

"I'm not going to poke at them. I just want to find out if they were hired to reanimate my target. It doesn't change an-ything even if I know for sure, but I'm curious."

"Rachel said she'd get you your money anyway. I do un-derstand why you traveled all the way back there, though. I'd be curious, too. I did a little research after Rachel told me what happened. Did you know there are only two necromancers in the city? Well, two who really matter. There's a handful of others, but they can't do full reanimations."

"I don't need you to look into it."

"Oh, I wanted to. I find all of this hilarious. I've been snick-ering every time I think about it since Rachel told me. I wish I could've been there to see your face when she told you that your target was still alive."

He was still teasing, but Vale knew what Russell would have done if he *had* been there. He would have been just as pissed as Vale, and he would have tried to find a solution.

That was how the three of them worked. They were each other's family, and if one of them needed anything, the other two rushed to help. Vale was kind of surprised that Russell wasn't in town yet. It wasn't only because he wanted to help him but also because he was clearly curious about the necromancer.

Vale didn't blame him. He wanted to find out what the fuck had happened, too, and maybe meet this necromancer. He hoped to never need one, but it might be worth it to be friendly with him. At the very least, he didn't want them to become enemies.

"You would have seen me angry," Vale told Russell. "I'll keep you updated, all right?"

"Yeah. Be careful. I've met a necromancer or two in my life, and while I'm not saying they're all weird, most of them are. You don't know what you're in for, and from what I saw, the two main necromancers in the city are very powerful."

"And do my research before doing anything," Vale promised. It warmed his heart to hear Russell so worried about him. No one else but Rachel was, but that was enough for Vale.

He didn't need a bunch of people in his life. He just needed Russell and Rachel, and he had them.

They were more than enough.

Cyril might be a necromancer, but a lot of his life revolved around his phone. For some reason, even though he had an email and a website, his phone was how most of his clients tried to reach him. It probably had to do with the urgency of their situations, but sometimes Cyril wished he could drown his cell phone in the toilet.

He sighed and picked it up, sighed again when he didn't recognize the number, and put on the most professional tone he had. "Cyril Moreau, what can I do for you?"

"You're the necromancer?" a gruff voice asked.

"I'm *a* necromancer, yes. What can I do for you?"

"I want to hire you to permanently reanimate my father."

"Well, I can certainly hear you out. Why don't you give me some details?"

The man hesitated. "What kind of details?"

"Your name, to start."

There was even more hesitation, and Cyril wondered what was up with that. He'd only asked for the man's name. Surely, that wouldn't be a problem.

"Paul Walker."

Cyril sucked in a breath. He was wrong. The name was definitely a problem.

Everyone in the city knew the Walker family. Cyril didn't know if they were Mafia or whatever, but they were definitely organized crime. He didn't pay much attention to all that stuff, but he knew enough through his contacts to be aware of the drug dealing and crimes. He'd always stayed away from these people, and he hadn't changed his mind.

He wanted nothing to do with the Walker family. He definitely wanted nothing to do with James Walker, who he'd just heard on the news had died.

Cyril had been fiercely satisfied to find out that the man at the head of the crime family was gone. He lived in a safe neighborhood, so he hadn't been impacted much by what the family did, but when he was younger, he and his mother lived in parts of the city that weren't great. He'd seen crime, and he'd always been grateful to have his ability, because it meant he'd been able to pull himself and his mother out of there.

"I'm going to stop you right there," he quickly said. "My answer is no. I can't reanimate your father."

"You might want to rethink that answer."

There was a quiet threat in the man's voice that sent a shiver down Cyril's back. It would probably be smarter for him to say yes, but he couldn't. "I just did a full reanimation a few days ago, and I'm still recuperating from that.

Unfortunately, that means I don't have enough power to fully reanimate anyone else for a few weeks. By then, it will be too late for your father's body, unfortunately."

"You're lying."

"I'm not. I'm really sorry, Mr. Walker, both for your loss and for having to say no, but I can't work a full reanimation right now. I'm sure you'll find someone else to do so."

"You're the best."

Cyril didn't like the fact that the new head of the local crime family thought he was the best at this. They might want to use him right now, but he was sure they'd also want to kick his ass if he ever reanimated someone they'd killed. That was why he stayed as far away from them as possible.

He wasn't about to change that.

"Thank you, and while I agree, my answer is still no. There's no need for you to call again and try to change my mind. It's a permanent answer. Have a good day, sir."

Cyril hung up before the guy could say anything else. He stared at the phone in his hand for a moment longer and wondered what the fuck had happened and what he was supposed to do with this. He wished he could say he believed the phone call would be a one-off, but people rarely — if ever — said no to these people. He couldn't imagine what happened to those who did, but he'd just done it.

What would that mean for him? They couldn't very well kill him if they wanted him to work for them, but that didn't mean they couldn't hurt him. He'd have to be careful for the next few days, and hopefully, they didn't know where he lived. He'd made sure not to list his address anywhere because he didn't want any weirdo to find him. Besides, once the body had either been reanimated or was too far gone to be, he'd be all right.

He wasn't sure he could fully convince himself of that, but he was going to try.

"Did you see who died?"

Vale frowned as he reached for the remote control on the nightstand next to the bed. He was sitting against the headboard, trying to relax as he waited for Artemis's email. He'd been planning on researching the local necromancers, but Russell had called, and Vale couldn't avoid answering.

Russell had been talking for what felt like hours. He'd always been a talker, and while sometimes it annoyed Vale, other times it was soothing. It was almost as if Russell was in the hotel room with Vale. It really had been too long since they'd last seen each other.

He turned on the TV and looked for the news, but they were talking about other stuff, and he didn't have it in him to use his phone to check. "Who?"

"James Walker."

"Really? Who killed him?"

Vale and Russell knew of the Walker family. Everyone in their profession did. Vale had never had to deal with them, but Russell had, and he had stories. Vale was glad they'd never tried to hire him, but if they had, his answer would have been no.

Russell laughed. "No idea. Good riddance, though."

"I agree." His phone beeped, telling him he had another call. "I have to go. I'll call you again later," he promised.

"You'd better, or you'll find me waiting for you on your bed."

It was a threat Russell would follow up with, so Vale knew better than to break his promise.

He hung up with Russell and answered Artemis's phone call. "You have something else for me?"

"I do."

"Anything I need to know in particular?"

"I emailed you again with more info, but it's just a regular hit. Your target is male, forty-three, and I included a list of places where you can find him in the email. Let me know what you think after you read it, all right?" After he took a quick peek at the email, it sounded like a fairly easy job. The client was looking for someone to eliminate a man who sounded similar to Vale's last target.

"As long as it's as you say, it shouldn't be a problem. Have you heard the news about James Walker?"

"Yeah. The message boards are on fire talking about it."

"Do you know what happened to him? Did someone put out a hit on him?"

"If that's what happened, they didn't do it on the boards. I didn't know anything about it until I read that he was dead."

Vale supposed that even bad guys died of natural causes. He would have been surprised if that was the case here, but anything was possible.

"But the family is wealthy enough to hire a necromancer," Artemis continued.

Vale swore and sat up straighter. "You think they're going to try to hire one?"

"Unless his family had him killed, I wouldn't be surprised if they do. There are a few very good necromancers in the city."

It was none of Vale's business, but he'd been doing this job for a long time, and he knew things the general public wasn't aware of. It was a good thing that James Walker was dead, and it would be a bad one if he became reanimated. Everyone would benefit from him being dead, and he hoped his family was included in that *everyone*, but there was no way to know. "Let's hope not."

"I guess that even if they contact a necromancer, the necromancer could say no."

"Let's hope so." Vale didn't have anything against

necromancers, and he understood they had to earn money and live their lives, but he hated the thought of someone bringing back such an awful man.

But whatever necromancer they contacted might not have a choice. Vale didn't know much about the family beyond James Walker, but something told him that James's son and heir wouldn't take no for an answer.

Dammit. He'd been curious about the necromancer who'd reanimated his last target, but he was getting worried now. What if they were forced to reanimate James Walker?

Being involved with the Walker family was never a good thing, and it was a minor miracle that the two most powerful necromancers in the city had managed to avoid them until now. With James Walker dead, though, that might change.

Vale wasn't a protector, but he felt for them, even though he'd never met either necromancer. They might be forced into doing something they didn't want, which should never happen. Beyond that, it would be better if James Walker stayed dead.

Unfortunately, Vale suspected that wouldn't be the case.

Chapter Four

Vale felt a sense of déjà vu as he followed his target into a motel. What was it with middle-aged men coming to these places? At least this motel was nicer than the last one, but not by much.

This place smelled of perfume instead of dust and cigarette smoke, and the carpets were slightly less threadbare, but the windows weren't clean, and Vale had noticed the overgrown hedges and withered plants outside. There was a crack in the ceiling, and Vale could see dead flies stuck in the lamps.

His target didn't seem to care about any of that. That was probably because his attention was focused on a young woman with long dark hair. She'd been hovering by the elevators, but as soon as she saw him, she rushed to his side. When she reached for him, he quickly looked around and stepped away. It was almost as if he was afraid someone would notice them.

Vale didn't have to try very hard to guess what was happening here. If he had to guess, this man's wife had found out he was cheating and wanted him taken care of. She could probably easily divorce him, but she'd chosen to hire a professional killer instead, and who was Vale to refuse? He trusted Artemis. She would have looked into who this man was before reaching out to Vale. She knew he didn't kill people who he didn't feel deserved it, so there had to be more to the story than just cheating, but it was none of Vale's business.

The woman and the target were quietly talking. Vale noticed her slip a room key to the man, but they didn't go to the elevator together. The target said something to her, and she frowned but eventually nodded. She didn't look happy when the target moved toward the elevator while she stayed behind.

Vale quickly joined the target by the elevator door. The man was doing his best not to look at the woman, who looked both sad and like she wanted to strangle him. When she looked up, Vale caught her eye, and he winked at her.

The scowl his target gave him was amusing. Vale wasn't quite sure what was happening, but while he and his target walked into the elevator, the woman didn't. Had the idiot asked her to wait so it wouldn't look like they were going to the same room? If that was what he'd done, he should have been more discreet earlier. The woman had given him a key, for fuck's sake. Anyone looking their way would know what was happening, even though the woman had stayed behind.

The target was still glaring at Vale, but Vale acted as if he couldn't see him. He wouldn't be glaring for long, anyway.

The target didn't seem to notice that Vale didn't push any button. He pressed the number two, and the elevator went up. When he stepped out, Vale followed. Vale was tempted to continue following him just to see how he reacted, but he didn't want the idiot to start screaming bloody murder, so he stopped in front of a door and patted his pockets as if he was looking for his key. Luckily for him, his target didn't go far and stopped a few doors down the hallway. He opened the door and stepped inside, and Vale moved quickly, rushing forward and pushing the man into the room. The man turned around, angry, but Vale didn't give him time to yell or demand to know what was happening.

He already had his gun out and raised it to the man's forehead as he slammed the door shut with his foot. One shot, and the man fell onto the carpet in the room.

That was it.

Vale hated the thought of scaring the poor woman who was still downstairs, but there was no way out of it. She'd be the one to find the body, and Vale would be long gone by the time she did. That meant he had to get to work quickly.

Luckily, there wasn't much for him to do. He took out his phone after putting his gun away, snapped a few pictures in which it was obvious that his target was dead, and returned his phone to his pocket.

He was out of the room only a few moments later and striding toward the stairs. The elevator was moving, maybe carrying up the woman who would find the body. Vale didn't wait to check. He took the stairs down, then quickly left the motel. He'd parked his rental car close by, and by the time the body would be found, the motel would be far behind.

He turned into the parking lot of a fast-food joint and parked there. Taking out his phone, he quickly sent the pictures he'd taken to Artemis. He didn't need to prove to her that he'd done the job, but considering what had happened last time, he wanted her to have proof in case something similar happened again.

He didn't think it would. What would be the odds of having a necromancer reanimate two of his targets? Vale was pretty sure they were close to zero, but he felt better once he'd sent off the pictures. Since he was there, he grabbed something to eat and headed back to his hotel.

Now that the job was out of the way, he could focus on the necromancer. Artemis had told him that she'd looked into what had happened, so maybe he'd call her once he was back in his room. She'd probably have more information for him, and even if she didn't, he could confirm he'd killed his target.

Vale's plans went out the window when he opened his door and realized someone was there. For a second, he tensed, ready to fight, but he didn't need to.

Russell grinned from Vale's bed. He'd taken off his shoes,

and he was leaning against the headboard and had his legs crossed at the ankles. He was watching TV, and his eyes glittered with mischief as he took in Vale and the bag he was holding.

"You brought me lunch," he said as he threw the remote control on the bed. "You shouldn't have."

"I didn't," Vale said as he closed the door. "I didn't know you'd be here."

"But if you had, you *would* have brought me lunch, right?"

Vale acted as if he was thinking about it, then shook his head. "No."

"You wound me."

"If I did, you wouldn't be bothering me. What are you doing here, Russell?"

Russell slid to the edge of the mattress. "I'm here for the necromancer."

Of course he was. Russell liked everything weird, and necromancers were definitely weird. Vale wasn't surprised that Russell had latched on to what was happening, and he was glad to see him, even though they were already teasing each other.

He dumped the bag containing his food onto the desk. "I might be convinced to share my fries if you don't bother me too much," he told Russell as Russell barreled into him.

Their hug was intense. It had been too long since they'd last seen each other, and even though Vale acted grumpy, he was glad to see his friend.

"It's good to see you," Russell said as he pushed Vale away and grabbed the bag with the food. "I'm so happy to see you I might even share my fries."

Vale rolled his eyes and grabbed for the bag, but Russell danced away. Vale had missed Russell, but that feeling would only last for a few hours, if even that. Then Russell would start being annoying. What was he thinking the day they'd become friends?

He joined Russell on the bed after washing up in the bathroom. The food was spread out on the bag Russell had torn open. He'd split everything in half and was watching TV again, but he patted the mattress, silently telling Vale to park his ass there.

Vale sighed. He could already tell that Russell had questions, and he'd want Vale to answer all of them. Vale supposed it would be a good way for him to go over the information he had about the necromancer and help him decide what his next step would be.

With a sigh, he relaxed next to Russell and grabbed a fry. "I know you looked into the necromancers. What did you find?"

Cyril was at the grocery store with his mother when his phone rang. She glared at him and gestured at the bottled water, but he stuck his tongue out as he slid his phone from his pocket. "You can drink the water from your faucet."

"It tastes weird."

Cyril shrugged and answered the call. "Cyril Moreau, how can I help you?"

The man on the other side sucked in a breath. For a moment, Cyril wondered if it was the Walker family again. They'd called him a few times since that first call, and every time he realized it was them, he hung up. He wasn't sure what they were trying to do, but it made him nervous. Thankfully they'd have to stop soon because the body would be too degraded for him to do anything with it.

"I found your number on your website."

"You were looking for a necromancer?"

"Yes. It's for my brother."

Cyril relaxed, but there was still a chance it was the Walker family. "Why don't you tell me your name?"

"Of course. I apologize."

"There's nothing to apologize for. If you're calling me, it means you lost someone, and I understand these can be trying times."

"I'm George Franks. My brother William was just killed."

"I'm sorry for your loss."

"Yes, thank you. I'd like to talk to you about reanimating him."

"You said he just died?"

"As far as I can tell, it just happened." Mr. Franks hesitated. "I haven't called the police."

"That's fine." He would have to eventually, but Cyril hoped he'd be able to do his job and get out of there before the cops arrived. They'd want to talk to Mr. Franks's brother, but that had nothing to do with Cyril. With his luck, Detective Anderson would be assigned to the case, and that wasn't something he wanted to deal with.

He turned to his mother. "I'm sorry, I have to go," he whispered.

She nodded and waved him off. They'd been grocery shopping together, and he'd grabbed a few things for himself, but knowing her, she'd take everything to his apartment. She'd even make sure that what needed to go into the fridge went into the fridge and would probably play with Oscar for a bit.

Cyril quickly left the grocery store. Mr. Franks was still talking, but he wasn't giving Cyril much of the information he needed. That was normal. When people lost a loved one, they were all over the place, even when they made the decision to reanimate them.

He slid into the driver seat of his car and quickly grabbed his notepad and pen. "Can we start again from the beginning? I apologize, but I was at the grocery store."

"What do you need to know?"

"How recently did he die?"

"A few hours." Mr. Franks paused. "I'm with his body right now."

Cyril winced. That couldn't be easy. "I'm sorry. I can join you wherever you are."

Cyril didn't recognize the address Mr. Franks gave him, but Mr. Franks told him it was a motel. That wasn't a surprise. More often than not, when Cyril was called, it was straight to where the person he was supposed to reanimate had died. When their family members found them, they didn't want to move them, so they called right away for him. That was a good thing because it meant nothing could be messed up before he arrived.

"How did your brother die?"

"He was shot."

Cyril didn't like this. "Where?"

"In the head. The center of the forehead."

That reminded him of the last reanimation he'd done. That man had been shot in the forehead, too. The wife had paid Cyril for a full reanimation then, and while he hoped that wasn't what would happen today, something told him he shouldn't hope too hard.

"I have to warn you about head wounds," he said. "I can reanimate your brother, but his personality might be different, and he might be missing memories. It all depends on what the bullet ruined as it went through him."

Mr. Franks swallowed heavily. "That's fine. I still want to try."

"I can give you the names of a few healers who will be able to help you once I'm done. What kind of reanimation are we talking about?"

"Full. I can pay."

That wasn't what worried Cyril. "That should be fine, although I can't make promises until I see the body. I'll be there as soon as I can, so please, don't let anyone touch him."

"I won't. I didn't tell anyone what happened, and there's only one other person who knows."

"I'll be there quickly."

Luckily for Mr. Franks, the motel wasn't far. Cyril didn't look around as he parked his car and grabbed his bag from the trunk. He was already focused on the job and what he would have to do.

If anyone had asked him, he wouldn't have been able to explain how reanimations worked. It was just something his body knew how to do, and he did it easily. He always had. It had started with a fly, and now he could do full reanimations. He knew just how much energy to give the bodies so that they could continue living a full and happy life. The younger the person he was reanimating, the more power he had to use, but even then, he could generally do a full reanimation a week. That was far more than what most necromancers were capable of, and he'd always been proud of that.

Mr. Franks had given Cyril a room number, so he headed there without stopping at the front desk. No one tried to stop him. It didn't look like anyone knew someone had been shot in the building, which was a relief because it meant Cyril wouldn't have to deal with cops.

He took the elevator up to the second floor and found the right room. He'd barely knocked before the door flew open, and a middle-aged man with red eyes and a crooked tie waved him in.

"Cyril Moreau?" the man asked.

"Mr. Franks?"

The man's shoulders slumped as he nodded. "That's me. He's still on the floor. I didn't touch him."

A whimper caught Cyril's attention. He looked at the armchair by the window to see that a young woman was sitting there. Her makeup had disintegrated from all her crying, and she was clutching a tissue against her mouth. Her focus was on the body on the floor, and even though she blinked, she never looked away.

"I'm sorry for your loss," Cyril whispered.

Mr. Franks didn't even look at the woman. "Thank you. What can you do for my brother?"

Cyril wanted to ask more questions, but he reminded himself that what had happened and who these people were was none of his business. He was here to do a job, and he would do it.

He set down his bag and crouched next to the body. He sent out a tendril of power, satisfied when he realized that Mr. Franks had been honest. His brother had only been dead for a little while, which would make the reanimation easier.

Cyril got back to his feet and faced Mr. Franks. "As I'm sure you know, a full reanimation isn't cheap."

"That's not a problem. Just tell me where I need to send you the money."

Thankfully, technology was on Cyril's side. Within a few minutes, he'd given Mr. Franks all his details, and the money had been transferred to his bank account. Mr. Franks hadn't even hesitated. He kept glancing at his brother as if he couldn't look away.

Cyril was used to working with people watching him, so it didn't bother him. He took out a few things from his bag and cleaned the wound on the dead man's forehead. He explained to Mr. Franks and the woman that he wouldn't be able to heal the wound, and as promised, he gave them the names of a few people who could help them with that. His focus would be on the reanimation. He didn't heal people.

The fresher a body was, the easier reanimation was. This was a full reanimation, and the amount of power that Cyril had to drain from his own body to make it work reminded him that he'd worked another one recently. He might have to take a vacation once this was finished. He was tired, but thankfully, it was nothing he couldn't deal with today. The dead Mr. Franks was middle-aged, so Cyril wouldn't have to use as much as he would have if the man had been in his twenties.

He pushed his power into the dead Mr. Franks as he began the reanimation. The dead man sucked in a breath, and his eyes opened. The woman in the armchair screeched, but she didn't come closer. The alive Mr. Franks did, though, crouching over his brother's body.

"You're a dumb ass," he said.

There was affection in his tone, and Cyril was tempted to ask why he was saying that to his brother. Clearly, the Mr. Franks who'd been killed had pissed someone off.

The previously dead Mr. Franks blinked. "What?"

"Did you really think she wasn't going to kill you when she found out you had a mistress? You know her. She had you killed, and your girl called me in hysterics when she found you like this."

The previously dead Mr. Franks croaked and tried to sit up. Cyril helped him, then quickly grabbed his bag and stepped away. Whatever happened next would be none of his business.

He cleared his throat. "I'm going to go."

Neither of the Mr. Franks looked at him. The woman didn't, either. She was staring at the man who had previously been dead with wide eyes.

Cyril left the room, and still, no one noticed him.

Even though Vale's necromancer troubles weren't over yet, it was easier for him to relax when he was with Russell. They were both professional killers, but they both forgot about the job when they were relaxing over a good steak, drinking beer, and behaving as if everything was right in the world. Russell was talking, gesturing with his hands as he did so, and Vale still wasn't getting annoyed listening to him.

He'd missed his friend, even though he would never admit that to Russell.

Vale's phone vibrated in his pocket. He took it out, smiling when he saw it was Rachel. "Hey. Russell and I are having dinner together, and we miss you. We should really organize something."

"It happened again."

Her tone was enough to tell Vale this was a work call. He sat up and frowned. "What do you mean? What happened again?" he had to be careful what he said since they were in a restaurant, but he wanted answers.

"Your target was reanimated. I got a call from the client, and she was hysterical. She yelled at me because her husband was still alive."

Russell had leaned closer so he could listen in to the conversation. He barked out a laugh, and when Vale glared at him, he pressed his lips together. It was clear he was trying very hard not to laugh, but not Vale. No, Vale wanted to find the necromancer and strangle them.

"You got my pictures, right?" he asked Artemis.

"I did, and I emailed them to the client as soon as I got them. She says it doesn't count because she paid to have a dead husband, and hers is alive."

"Did you tell her to fuck off?"

"I did, and I already wired the money into your account, so you don't have to worry about that."

"No, I only have to worry about this fucking necromancer. Why does it feel like they're doing this to annoy me?"

"I would if it was me," Russell said.

Vale glared at him harder. He mimed for Russell to shut his mouth, and Russell mimed locking his lips together and throwing away the key.

As if that would be enough to make him shut up.

"I need to know what happened," Vale said. "I'm not taking any more jobs in this city."

"I'm tempted not to give you any more jobs in the city anyway. This is a mess, Roux."

Vale winced at his work name. Russell had come up with it, and every time someone used it, Vale cringed. Russell had precisely zero creativity. Vale had blond hair, but he'd died it red for a job once at the beginning of his career, so of course, Russell had started calling him the French word for ginger. Unfortunately, the name had stuck and that was how Vale had been known in the message boards and to clients ever since.

"Now that the job's done, I'll look more into the necromancer," Vale promised.

"I'll help," Russell volunteered. "I think it's hilarious, but I'm also curious about the necromancer. The guy has to be rich if he continues doing this kind of job. Are the reanimations permanent?"

Vale glared at him. "Who cares?" He certainly didn't. He'd done his job and had been paid for it, and that was it for him. He wanted nothing to do with his target or the man's wife ever again.

"Let me know what you find," Artemis said. "I don't want this person to continue ruining our job."

"You can't kill them," Vale warned.

"Are you sure? I can't even hire you or Russell to kill them?"

"They're just doing their job, just like you and I."

Maybe Vale should talk to the necromancer, though. It had to be a coincidence, unless the necromancer knew who Vale was and was coming after him on purpose, but Vale couldn't imagine how that could be possible. He didn't know anyone in the city, especially not a necromancer. No one would have any reason to do something like this to him.

But he wasn't willing to risk it a third time.

CHAPTER FIVE

Cyril had left the grocery store so quickly the other day that he'd had to come back today to grab more stuff. His fridge was empty again, and his stomach had reminded him loudly of that when he'd opened it to grab something for lunch. His breakfast hadn't been great, either, but that was something he could deal with. He had to eat lunch, though, which was why he was back at the store without his mother this time.

He was distracted as he pushed his cart out of the store. He unloaded everything into the trunk of his car, returned the cart, and moved back toward his car. He'd bought everything to make himself a BLT sandwich for lunch, and he couldn't wait.

Movement caught his attention, and he turned toward a van just in time for a man to grab his arm. He tried pulling away, frantically looking around for someone who would help him, but the parking lot was empty.

"What are you doing? Let me go!"

The man didn't let him go—not that Cyril had expected him to. He remembered reading somewhere never to allow a kidnapper to pull you into a vehicle, and he had no intention of following this guy into the van or anywhere else.

He grabbed the nearest car, hanging on to the side mirror as the man tried to pull him forward. The man growled and pulled harder, but Cyril wasn't moving. He would hug the side mirror until the guy let him go.

"What the hell is going on here?"

The man finally let go of Cyril and turned to look at the

newcomer. Cyril turned to run, but another man appeared in front of him. The three strangers wore suits, although it was clear that the suit on the man who'd spoken was of a much better quality. The other two looked like they could be body-guards.

Cyril looked from one to the other, then back to the grocery store doors. Someone had to come out eventually, right?

But he'd been dragged toward the edge of the parking lot, away from the grocery store and the road. Someone would probably notice him eventually, but these three guys could do a lot of damage before it happened.

Cyril raised his hands. "Look, I can give you my cell phone and wallet. I won't scream, and I won't tell anyone what happened."

The man who'd spoken looked unimpressed. He had to be in his fifties, with hair that was almost entirely white at his temples. The rest was still dark, though, and it gave him a distinguished air. His suit was well-tailored, and he was way too elegant for a grocery store parking lot.

The man took out a packet of cigarettes. He slid one out and stuck it into his mouth.

Cyril wrinkled his nose. "Those will kill you," he warned.

The man didn't seem to care. He lit the cigarette and took a long drag, then blew the smoke in Cyril's direction. "Will they? Well, that wouldn't be a problem if I had you close by to reanimate me, would it?"

Cyril swallowed. He wasn't surprised to find out that this had to do with his job.

He tried to be careful about whom he agreed to reanimate, but it was hard for him to find out who the people he worked with were and what they'd done to be killed. Sometimes his reanimations made people angry.

"If you wanted to hire me for a job, there are easier ways to do so."

"Like calling you? We tried that several times, but you've said no every time."

Cyril disliked every part of this. "Did I?"

The man took another drag of his cigarette. "James Walker."

Cyril had *known* he wouldn't like this. "I'm sorry, but no. I've already told James Walker's son that I couldn't reanimate him, and I stand by that."

The man stared at Cyril. Cyril didn't think this guy was James Walker's son. He was too old. From what little he knew, James Walker had been in his sixties.

"How much money do you want?" the man asked.

"It's not a matter of money. It's a matter of who James Walker was."

The man's expression tightened. "So you're telling me that no matter what we offer, you won't do it?"

"Precisely. I'm really sorry, but I choose who I reanimate as carefully as I can. Everyone in the city knows who James Walker was. I have no intention of bringing him back, considering everything he's done."

One of the other two men stepped closer to Cyril. Cyril sighed, already knowing what was about to happen. At the very least, he'd be beaten up. At the worst, he'd be killed.

But no. If they wanted him to reanimate James Walker, they couldn't kill him. They could hurt him, which they probably would, but at least he'd get out of this alive.

And hopefully, in one piece.

Vale was impressed. He'd expected the necromancer to give in once he realized what was happening, but the man was standing his ground. He'd told Walker's people that he wouldn't reanimate Walker, and that was that.

It was clear from the necromancer's expression that he

knew what was about to happen. These three wouldn't kill him, but they *would* hurt him. They'd found out they couldn't buy Cyril to make him do what they wanted, so now, they would move on to other tactics. People like this only understood two things—money and pain.

When Vale had located the necromancer, he'd had no idea what to expect. Like Russell had said, there were only two necromancers strong enough to do two full reanimations so close together in the area, so he'd had a fifty-fifty chance of finding the right one. It hadn't been hard. He'd looked into his past two targets and had discovered who their families had hired to bring them back to life.

Cyril Moreau.

With a name like that, his father had to have French origins. Vale was curious. How had Cyril become a necromancer? Did it come from his mother's side of the family or his father's?

More than that, Vale was curious about what kind of person Cyril was. He was standing up to Walker's goons, even though, from where Vale stood, he could see Cyril was terrified.

He shouldn't step in. He'd looked into Cyril because he wanted to know more about the necromancer who kept reanimating his targets, but what was happening was none of his business. He didn't have a horse in this race, even though he didn't want James Walker to be reanimated. He should stay far away and let Cyril deal with this, but he could already see how it would end, and he didn't want the necromancer to be hurt. Cyril had only been doing his job. He'd been hired to reanimate two of Vale's targets permanently, and he'd done it. He didn't know who Vale was or what he did for a living. He didn't know those had been Vale's targets.

With a sigh, Vale pushed away from his car. It made sense that Cyril hadn't noticed him, since he was half-hidden behind a van, but the other three? Considering who they worked for, they should have been more careful. They should have seen Vale as soon as they arrived in the parking lot, but instead, he'd been the one to see them. When he'd realized they were staring at Cyril as he walked out of the grocery store, he'd known what was about to happen.

He was right.

One of the goons had cut off Cyril's escape route. The other still stood next to the third man, who seemed to be in charge. The goons both looked at their boss, waiting for his orders, but Vale had already had enough. The sooner this mess was over, the sooner he could go back to his hotel room and start planning his trip home.

He moved closer and cleared his throat to get everyone's attention. The guy in charge narrowed his eyes at him, but he didn't know Vale, so he had no idea what was about to happen. None of them did.

Vale plastered a smile on his face. "You weren't about to beat him up, were you?" he asked.

"It's best if you walk away, unless you want the same thing to happen to you," the guy in charge said. He threw his cigarette on the ground and stomped on it.

Vale tsked. "I should have known you didn't care about keeping our world clean. You wouldn't, considering who you work for."

"Take care of him," the guy barked.

The two goons rushed toward Vale at the same time. It had been a while since he'd fought this kind of fight. Usually he killed his targets quickly, which meant they didn't have time to fight him. He knew what he was doing, though. He might not usually use his fists, but he still knew what to do with them.

He grabbed the first guy who reached him and turned him around, plastering the guy's back against his chest. When the other reached them, he tried to punch Vale, but Vale pushed the first guy against him. They crashed together, losing their balance. As they went down, Vale grabbed the one closer to him, hauled him up, and punched him in the nose. The guy went down like a sack of potatoes while the other scrambled to get back to his feet.

Vale kicked the man's legs from under him. He fell on top of the other, but he wasn't out. Neither of them were, which was a pity because it meant they would get back to their feet.

Vale cracked his knuckles and glanced toward the grocery store. For now, no one had noticed them, but that was bound to change.

"Idiots," the guy in charge muttered. "This isn't over, necromancer. You *will* reanimate James Walker."

Cyril had been watching all of this with wide eyes. His back was pressed against a blue car, and he looked like he didn't know what to do. He probably had no idea what was happening. Vale hadn't even introduced himself.

"I won't," he said in a trembling voice. "He doesn't deserve to be reanimated."

Damn, the man had balls. Even after everything that had just happened, he'd told the Walker family to fuck off.

The guy in charge didn't answer. He strode off, and the other two quickly scrambled to follow him. Vale watched them for a while, even though he knew they wouldn't return. They wouldn't want to attract too much attention in a public place, especially after Vale had kicked their asses. They'd probably try to look into him, but since they couldn't link him to the necromancer, it would be hard for them to find out who he was.

Vale was relieved they were leaving. He could have kicked their asses, but he didn't want to make a mess in a grocery store parking lot.

As soon as they were out of sight, he turned to Cyril. The man was still visibly shaky, but he pushed away from the car and closer to Vale. "I don't know how to thank you."

Vale shrugged. "You don't have to. It truly was a pleasure to kick those assholes around a bit. I knew they wouldn't do much since we're in such a public place."

"Still. They would have hurt me if it weren't for you. Thank you."

"Do you need help walking back to your car? You don't look like you should be driving."

"I'm fine. I'll just sit in my car for a few minutes and drink some water." Cyril hesitated. "Is there anything I can do to thank you?"

Vale crossed his arms over his chest. "Actually, there is. You can tell me why you keep reanimating my targets."

Cyril couldn't make sense of the words. What did this guy mean? Who were his targets? "I'm sorry?"

"You did it twice now. I killed my targets, and you reanimated them. You *fully* reanimated them, which means my clients are pissed and trying not to pay me. It's getting annoying."

Cyril sucked in a breath. The last two reanimations he'd worked on had both been killed by a single shot in the middle of the forehead. Was this guy saying he was the one who'd killed them?

Shit. If he'd killed them, he had to be pissed with Cyril for reanimating them. This was clearly his job, and Cyril was threatening his livelihood.

What the fuck was happening? If this guy was a professional killer, why had he helped Cyril with the Walker family? Wouldn't it have been better for him to let them hurt him? Instead, he'd stopped them and kept Cyril safe.

Or at least Cyril *appeared* to be safe. If this guy was a professional killer, Cyril doubted he was.

He turned and tried to run. The guy was alone—Cyril

hoped so anyway—and there was no one to cut his escape route. Unfortunately for Cyril, the guy was fast. He grabbed Cyril's arm and pulled him back, making Cyril stumble. He hit the closest car and scrambled to stay on his feet.

"Please. I swear I won't reanimate your—your targets again. I didn't know they were your targets, and I only reanimated them because I was paid to do so. It's nothing against you, I swear. I didn't know you existed until now."

To Cyril's surprise, the guy let go of Cyril and raised both his hands. It was as if he was showing Cyril that he wasn't dangerous, which Cyril didn't understand.

Of course the guy was dangerous. He'd told Cyril he was a professional killer. He could probably kill Cyril in three different ways right now without even breaking a sweat.

"I didn't mean to scare you," the man said.

Cyril couldn't help it—he snorted loudly. He slapped a hand over his mouth, hoping the professional killer staring at him wouldn't be offended by his reaction. He fully expected to be threatened, but instead, the man smiled.

Before finding out what the man's profession was, Cyril had noticed how handsome he was. His dark blond hair was cut short, and his brown eyes seemed to take in everything in the area. He was in his late thirties, tall, and well-built. That made sense if his job was as physical as Cyril suspected. He was even more handsome now that he was smiling, but Cyril wondered if the smile should be taken as a threat. The man hadn't had any trouble with the two suits who had attacked him. He'd be able to tear Cyril in half without even a thought.

"I'm not here to hurt you," the man said, his rumbling voice making Cyril shiver.

"You just told me you were a professional killer."

"And I just saved you from Walker's goons. I'm not here to hurt you," he repeated.

Cyril wasn't sure he could believe him, but he wanted to.

When had his life become so messy? He just wanted to do his job, spend time with his mother and Oscar, and have a peaceful life. He'd known that wouldn't be possible since he was a necromancer, but he'd done his best to stay away from any complications or people who would try to use him for their gain. So far, he'd managed, but now that the Walker family had latched onto him, he had to be careful. They hadn't taken his refusal to reanimate James Walker well, and they'd be dangerous even after the man's body was too degraded to be reanimated. Cyril suspected they'd hold a grudge, and he wasn't sure how to deal with it.

"Why are you here, then?" he asked, tempted to make a run for it again. The grocery store parking lot was still empty. Was everyone still shopping inside? How much food did they need?

"I told you," the assassin said with a crooked smile. "I just want you to stop reanimating my targets."

"And how am I supposed to know they're your targets? It's not like they have your name written on their forehead." Cyril sucked in a breath. "Although they were killed the same way."

The assassin nodded. "It was the easiest and fastest way."

"So am I not supposed to reanimate anyone who's been shot in the head?"

The man looked frustrated, so Cyril wasn't surprised when he reached for him again. He flinched and pressed his back harder against the car behind him, trying to put more distance between them. For some reason, the man frowned.

Surely he had to realize that Cyril was terrified of him. He'd admitted to being a professional killer and to killing at least two people recently. How was Cyril supposed to feel? How could he be anything but terrified?

"Fine," he spat out. "I'll stop reanimating anyone who's been shot in the forehead. Is that all right with you? Is it enough?"

Cyril needed to get out of here, dammit. He had to leave before this guy changed his mind and hurt him.

Vale felt like a monster. What had he expected to happen when he told Cyril that he was a professional killer? The man was afraid of him. Vale had beaten up two guys in front of him, told him he killed people for a living, and demanded he stop reanimating the people he killed. Cyril was right when he said there was no way for him to know who Vale had killed. It wasn't like Vale only used his gun in his line of work. It was what he preferred, but it didn't always work that way.

"Please," Cyril continued. "I'll do whatever you want. I don't want to die."

Vale hated that he'd frightened Cyril so badly. The man was small and cute, and Vale had never meant to be threatening. He just wanted to talk, but he could see now that telling Cyril that he was a professional killer wasn't the best way to go about it.

He sighed. "Let's try this again from the beginning, all right? I'm Vale."

Cyril stared with wide eyes. He didn't say anything, so Vale continued.

"I know who you are, Cyril. You're one of the best necromancers in the city, if not *the* best. That's why James Walker's family is coming after you. There's no one better than you to reanimate him. It's also why you were hired to reanimate my last two targets. You're good at what you do, just like I am."

Cyril pressed his lips together. "Is that a threat?"

How was Vale messing things up so badly? "It's not." He looked around and noticed a coffee shop close by. "Why don't we go sit down and get a coffee? We can talk in a public place, so you can be sure I won't hurt you. That's all I want."

Cyril didn't look convinced. "Why do you want to talk to me? Do you want to hire me to reanimate someone?"

"No. My job is to kill people, not reanimate them. I don't want anything from you beyond a conversation, I swear."

Cyril glanced back toward the grocery store. A woman with a child had come out and was pushing her cart toward a car. Vale was pretty sure that Cyril was considering screaming for help, but what could the woman do? Especially with a young child to protect? Cyril didn't trust Vale, which was understandable. He probably expected Vale to kill anyone who tried to stop him from talking to him.

Cyril nodded stiffly. "We can get coffee."

Vale hoped it would be enough. He wanted Cyril to understand that he wasn't here to hurt him or even threaten him. He was just curious about him and what had happened with his targets.

He gestured toward the coffee shop. "Let's go, then."

Cyril moved forward. Vale quickly started walking next to him, not wanting him to think he'd kill him from behind if he stayed back. He kept an eye on the parking lot and the road, just in case, but Walker's men were gone.

Vale and Cyril made it to the coffee shop without incident. Cyril looked like he was about to bolt, but he didn't. Instead, as soon as they were inside, he went to flop into a chair at one of the tables.

Vale arched a brow, amused. "Are you telling me I'm supposed to buy you coffee?"

"You're the one who wanted to talk in a coffee shop. I'll take a chai tea, small, with coconut milk."

Vale was impressed by how normal Cyril sounded. A lot of people would have been cowering and trying to be cooperative, but not Cyril. He could probably tell that Vale wouldn't hurt him, but he still knew what Vale did for a living and how easy it would be for him to kill him. Yet he still had demands and didn't look afraid to make them.

"I'll be right back," Vale promised.

He headed toward the back of the store to get their drinks. He kept an eye on Cyril, but the man didn't even take out his phone. He was staring ahead, frowning as if he was trying to make sense of something, probably of Vale. It wasn't every day that Vale told someone what he did for a living and protected them at the same time.

His phone vibrated right after he gave the woman behind the counter his order. He slid the phone out, not surprised to see Russell had texted him. He'd been pouting when Vale had left the hotel room because he'd wanted to — as he'd said — go on this adventure with him, but Vale had told him to stay put. Vale was intimidating enough on his own without adding Russell to the mix.

Vale quickly texted back, then took the drinks when his name was called. He turned toward the table where Cyril had sat down, but his chair was empty.

Vale looked around. Cyril was nowhere to be found.

"He left," a woman sitting at the table next to the one Cyril had chosen said. "Sorry, you were stood up for that date."

Vale shrugged. "It's fine."

The woman eyed him, and since he didn't want the situation to become even messier, he nodded at her and left the coffee shop. He hoped Russell liked chai tea with coconut milk, but maybe he should take the drink to Cyril.

He was impressed by Cyril. Even more than that, he was intrigued. When he'd found out everything Cyril had done and how powerful he was, he'd expected someone hard, who wouldn't have a problem fighting the three men demanding he reanimate someone who was better off dead. Instead, Cyril was small and soft. He was good at his job and too sweet to be a necromancer.

This wouldn't end well for him. The Walker family had

noticed him, and from what Vale knew about them, they wouldn't stop until they got what they wanted. James Walker might be dead, but someone else was in charge of the family now, probably his son. They would continue coming after Cyril until he did what they asked, and even if he did, they wouldn't let him go. Cyril was too useful, especially to such a powerful crime family.

The necromancer was in trouble, and while it was none of Vale's business and he knew he should stay out of it, he couldn't.

CHAPTER SIX

Cyril was surprised that he remembered to take the groceries out of his trunk once he arrived home. The only thing he wanted to do was rush inside his apartment, lock the door and every window, and hide.

The Walker family was angry at him. A professional assassin had asked him to stop reanimating his targets.

What the fuck was happening?

Cyril rushed inside, laden with bags. He hadn't wanted to make a second trip, so he was carrying everything. As soon as he was in the apartment, he slammed the door shut, dumped all of the bags on the floor, and locked the door. He stared at it for a moment before moving a chair in front of it.

There. No one would be coming in from there.

Or maybe they would. Cyril had no idea what kind of things a professional assassin could do beyond killing. Vale had clearly been trained, though. He'd kicked the asses of those two Walker family assholes without even breaking a sweat while Cyril had been cowering in a corner.

He picked up his bags and headed to the kitchen, where he checked the window. It was locked, too. He always locked the windows when he left the apartment, and he'd never been so glad that he'd updated the air conditioning last year. It meant he didn't need to open the windows, even though it was July.

He put away all of his groceries before flopping into his favorite armchair. He toed off his shoes and stretched out his legs, sighing in relief. When he heard the ticking sound of Oscar coming toward him, he smiled. He'd wondered where his baby was.

Oscar climbed up the side of the armchair and flopped into Cyril's lap. Cyril rubbed a hand over Oscar's smooth body, telling himself to relax. He was home. He was safe, and no one could find him. Even if they could, they couldn't get to him. He was in his apartment.

"What the fuck is that thing?" someone asked from a dark corner of the living room.

Cyril recognized the voice in an instant. He jumped to his feet and screamed as he threw Oscar toward the voice. He regretted it seconds later, but it was too late. Vale had already grabbed Oscar as if Cyril had thrown him a ball. Oscar's tentacles waved around as he tried to use them to scratch Vale, but Vale was keeping him at arm's length. That didn't stop Oscar. When he realized he couldn't touch Vale's face, he wrapped his tentacles around Vale's forearms.

That was when Vale's composure broke. Until now, he'd been a hard professional assassin, but Oscar seemed to be the straw that broke the camel's back. Vale swore and tried to shake him off, but he couldn't. Oscar latched onto him. He was clinging to Vale's forearms and trying to get closer to his face, even though he wouldn't be able to do much if he reached it. He was fiercely defensive of Cyril.

Vale turned to Cyril. "Please get it off me."

Cyril didn't know how he felt. He was terrified that Vale had come to kill him, but at the same time, watching the big bad professional assassin freaking out over Oscar was hilarious. Oscar wouldn't hurt a fly. He was weird, and people were wary of him because of that, but it didn't make him dangerous.

Cyril giggled, then slapped a hand against his lips. He looked at Vale with wide eyes, but Vale didn't seem to care that he was laughing. He was still trying to pry Oscar's tentacles off his forearms, looking a little bit wilder every time he managed to raise a tentacle, only for it to grab him again.

Cyril was still afraid, but how was he supposed to believe this guy was here to kill him when he couldn't even deal with Oscar?

What the fuck was this thing? Vale had no idea, but he wanted it off his body. The problem was that the thing was clinging to him. Every time Vale managed to raise one of its tentacles, it grabbed onto him with another.

It had eight.

Vale was starting to freak out. He'd seen a lot of odd things in his life, some of them terrifying, but nothing like this. Nothing like this bony creature trying to climb up his body, possibly to strangle him.

Another giggle caught Vale's attention. He looked up sharply to see that Cyril was staring at him with wide eyes, a hand pressed against his mouth as he laughed. He didn't seem at all worried about what was happening to Vale. Maybe it was because Vale had broken into his apartment, and Cyril wanted his demonic minion to kill him. Maybe the damn bony octopus answered to Cyril and would continue trying to climb up Vale's body until Cyril did something about it.

Vale shook out his arms, but the octopus clung on. Vale didn't know what else to call it, since it had eight legs and looked like an octopus, but not quite, since its body was made of *bones*. The central one that made up the main body of the octopus was a human skull. Its sockets were empty, but Vale could tell the thing was watching him.

It was fucking creepy.

"Can you do something about this?" Vale asked as he looked around for a weapon.

What could he use on this thing? It was already dead, so

killing it wouldn't help. That was the only thing Vale knew how to do, unfortunately. He was a killer at heart and by profession, and he didn't know how to deal with an already dead demon octopus.

Cyril rolled his eyes and reached for the tiny demon. He grabbed it without hesitation and, to Vale's astonishment, raised it to his chest to cuddle it.

"It's fine, baby," Cyril cooed. "He's not going to hurt me. Thank you so much for protecting me." Cyril scratched the top of the skull that made up the octopus's body.

Vale could only stare. "What the fuck is that?"

Cyril frowned at him. "Don't talk about Oscar like that."

"Oscar? Like *what*?"

"He's sensitive. Don't offend him just because you don't understand him."

Vale rubbed his face. What the fuck was he doing here? Why was he getting involved in this? Why did he care if Cyril lived or died?

At least that question was easy to answer. Vale thought Cyril was sweet and beautiful, and he didn't want him to die. Even if he'd been an asshole, he still wouldn't have deserved to be threatened by the Walker family. Vale wasn't usually a protector, but in this case, he wanted to be. He wanted to make Cyril smile and to ensure that the Walker family wouldn't get their dirty hands on him.

He was going nuts. That was the only way to explain this.

Vale cocked his head. *"What* is Oscar?"

Cyril shrugged and put his *thing* down onto the armchair. Oscar twisted around, his empty sockets looking in Vale's direction and making him want to run out the door or possibly a window if it was faster.

"He's my pet. What are you doing here? You broke into my apartment?"

Vale reached sideways and picked up the chai tea he'd

brought Cyril. It was a fresh one, because the first one had gotten cold. "You weren't there when I returned to the table, so I brought it to you."

Cyril stared at Vale and the tea in his hand for such a long time that Vale wondered what he was thinking. Then he quickly grabbed the tea from Vale's hand and took a sip, sighing in pleasure.

It didn't last long. Seconds later, Cyril was tense again.

"You broke into my apartment. How did you know where I live? It's not on my website, and I'm very careful not to give out my address."

"You do remember my profession, don't you? It was easy for me to find out where you live."

"Why are you here?"

Cyril was tense, and Vale wanted him to relax. He wasn't quite sure how to make that happen, but it would make what came next easier. "You still haven't told me what Oscar is."

"Does it matter?"

"Since he's going to haunt my nightmares, yes. Also, I like the name. Pretty clever."

Cyril smiled again. "You know French?"

"Not much, but enough to recognize that you named your bony pet *bone*." That was what the first two letters of Oscar's name meant in French. Considering that Oscar was a bunch of bones strung together by what Vale had to guess was necromancer magic, it was fitting.

"He really is my pet. I was lonely and put together a bunch of bones I had lying around."

"You were lonely and decided to create a monster?"

"Oscar isn't a monster. He's just misunderstood." Cyril's expression hardened. "Anyway, I want you out of my apartment."

"I know I shouldn't be here, but it's for your safety."

Cyril snorted. "My safety? You almost gave me a heart

attack and hurt my pet."

"How can I hurt your pet when he's a bunch of bones?"

"He has feelings!" Cyril said as he grabbed Oscar and clutched him against his chest.

The sight made Vale shudder. He'd touched Oscar, so he knew that his bones were smooth and warm, which was fucking creepy. He didn't know why Oscar was warm when he didn't have blood flow or flesh, and he wasn't sure he wanted to find out.

"I can't believe you," Cyril continued. "You not only break into my apartment, but you also make fun of my pet."

Vale could see they would go round and round with this conversation, which wasn't why he was here. He tried interrupting Cyril a few times, but the man glared at him and didn't hesitate to tell him what he thought of that. Vale would have to find another way.

As soon as Cyril had to stop talking to suck in a breath, Vale pressed a hand against his lips.

Blessed silence.

"I'm not here to hurt you," Vale said. "But you need to take the Walker family seriously."

Cyril raised Oscar toward Vale's face. Vale yelped and let go of Cyril, quickly stepping back and stumbling on the footrest. He almost fell but managed to catch himself on the wall.

Cyril snickered. He'd done it on purpose, the little shit.

Vale could tell Cyril was scared, but he was impressed by the way the necromancer was dealing with it. He might be terrified and upset, but he wasn't panicking, which was how this kind of situation usually went.

"What makes you think I don't take the Walker family seriously?" Cyril asked. "I'm not an idiot. I know how dangerous they are."

"Then you know you should leave town for a bit." Vale couldn't see another way out of this.

The Walker family wouldn't stop until they got what they wanted from Cyril, and they'd want more and more as time passed. For now, they wanted Cyril to reanimate James Walker, but what would happen if he did? They wouldn't let him go, because he was too useful. They'd keep him on a string like a puppet and take him out when they needed him, and he would have to do what they asked or risk being hurt.

Vale didn't want that for Cyril. He didn't want that for anyone, but especially not for the sweet and infuriating necromancer.

Cyril was angry, but he supposed anyone would be if a professional killer had broken into their apartment and insulted their pet. At least Vale had brought him tea. He hadn't had a chance to drink the first one Vale had bought, which was the only regret he had about running away.

Vale took a step forward, and Cyril quickly raised Oscar again. Vale eyed Oscar as if he expected him to bite, which was ridiculous. Oscar didn't have a beak like living octopi. On the other hand, he did have teeth, although most of them had fallen out a while ago. When Cyril had decided to try to create Oscar, he'd used whatever bones he had on hand. One of them had been a skull he'd found in a cemetery when he was fourteen that had been sitting on his desk since then. Oscar wouldn't do much biting with the three teeth left on the skull.

"You need to fuck off," Cyril told Vale. "I'm not going anywhere. I don't care what the Walker family wants from me. I'm not giving it to them, and I'm not allowing them to run me out of town."

Vale huffed in frustration. "Don't you see it would be the safest option for you? They're not going to stop coming after you."

"It won't be long before the body is too degraded for the

reanimation to happen. They'll leave me alone after that."

"Are you sure? Besides, they could have frozen the body, right?"

Cyril grimaced. He hated reanimating frozen people. He hated being cold, and frozen bodies were slow and weird. "I'll stay away from them."

"What if they don't want to stay away from you? Besides, this goes beyond James Walker. They know how powerful you are by now, which means they want to use you. Is that what you want? To have to work for the Walker family?"

Cyril pressed his lips together. He understood what Vale was saying, and he couldn't say it hadn't crossed his mind.

What would happen if he was forced to reanimate James Walker? He didn't want to do it, but he might have to. He wouldn't be surprised if the Walker family decided to keep him even if he did what they wanted. It was the kind of people they were. They used others, bent them to their will, and destroyed them once they were done with them.

Cyril wouldn't allow them to destroy him.

He stood up straighter and glared at Vale. "Thank you for the warning, but I can take care of myself."

Vale stared at Cyril for a moment.

Cyril wondered what was going on in his mind. He didn't understand Vale. As a professional killer, why was he worried about Cyril? He didn't have a reason to want Cyril dead, but he also shouldn't care whether Cyril lived or died. It wasn't like they were friends or even knew each other.

Yet Vale was here. He'd broken into Cyril's apartment to warn him about the Walker family. He'd brought him tea. He was a confusing man, and Cyril didn't like being confused. He already had to deal with enough of that in his profession.

Vale nodded. "All right. I wanted to warn you, and I did. You know what you're going against now, so I'll leave you be." He hesitated. "But be careful, all right?"

Cyril opened his mouth to tell him to fuck off again, but Vale was already turning toward the window. He quickly opened it and slid out, with Cyril staring after him.

"You couldn't have used the door?" he called out.

The only answer he got was a chuckle. He set Oscar down and rushed to the window, but when he leaned out, there were no signs of Vale. He'd vanished as if he'd never been there.

Cyril closed the window and locked it, then checked the lock just to be sure.

What the fuck was happening? Why was Vale so interested in him? People often were, but they were also afraid and wary. Cyril had seen none of that in Vale. No, the only thing that had scared Vale was Oscar, which Cyril thought was ridiculous. Oscar was a sweetheart.

Cyril went to flop into his armchair and picked up Oscar again, stroking his smooth head. "What the fuck am I going to do?" he asked out loud.

Oscar couldn't answer, but he snuggled close as if he understood that Cyril needed it.

Cyril was in trouble, wasn't he?

CHAPTER SEVEN

Vale should be on his way home by now. Hell, he should already be in his apartment, relaxing and waiting for Artemis to find another job for him.

Instead, he was still in his hotel room. At least Russell had booked one for himself, so they didn't have to share. Vale loved his friend, but he drew the line at sharing a room with him for more than a few days. He was tempted to strangle Russell after only a few hours, so who knew what would happen if they were forced to share living spaces for longer than that.

He tapped his fingertips on his thigh and stared at the TV. It was on, but he wasn't paying attention. He hadn't paid much attention over the past few days because his every thought had been focused on Cyril.

Why? Before, Vale had been able to tell himself that he was curious about Cyril. He'd never met a necromancer so powerful that he could fully reanimate two dead people over just a few weeks. Looking at Cyril, no one would guess he was capable of that. In fact, every time Vale saw Cyril, he had to resist the urge to coddle him. He'd been watching him from afar, making sure the Walker family stayed away from him, but he couldn't continue doing this forever. His life wasn't here, and he wasn't a bodyguard.

He was contemplating the option of hiring a bodyguard or two for Cyril when his phone rang. He checked the screen, relieved to see it wasn't Russell, and answered Rachel's phone call.

"Hey."

"You're not going to like what I have to tell you."

Vale could tell from Rachel's voice that this was a work call. He sat up straighter and frowned. "What is it?"

"I know you don't want any more jobs in the city, but I still keep an eye on jobs for you and Russell, so I noticed something popped up recently. It's not a hit, but a kidnapping."

Vale didn't like this. "Cyril?"

"Yeah. You mentioned him by name, and I recognized it. Someone wants to kidnap Cyril Moreau."

Vale swore. "It has to be the Walker family."

"I could look into it, but if I have to guess, I'd say you're right. What do you want to do about it? I know you don't take this kind of job and that even if you did, you wouldn't want it, but if I leave this up, someone else is going to take it."

Vale rubbed his face. "I have to go and talk to Cyril."

"You can certainly do that, but I don't know if it's going to help. You said he was kind of stubborn."

Was there a word for someone who was worse than stubborn? Mulish, maybe? "Can you do something to have the job taken down, even temporarily? I'll try and talk to Cyril."

"I'll do what I can, but I'm not making any promises. As far as I can tell, this is a legit job, and it's well-paid."

Vale didn't know what to do. This situation was completely new for him. He was good at going in, killing people, and leaving without looking back, but this was so very different. He didn't want Cyril to be hurt. He'd tried to warn him, but something told him that Cyril hadn't listened to him. He knew the Walker family was dangerous, but Vale didn't think he truly understood what they would do if they ever got their hands on him. He was probably galivanting around the city, going to the grocery store and working jobs without thinking twice about it.

He couldn't protect himself, which meant Vale would have

to protect him.

"Even if you can only give me a few hours, I'd be grateful," Vale said.

"I'll try to have it taken down entirely, but I don't know if I can do that. If you're going to keep him safe, you need to move now."

"I will."

He'd barely hung up when his phone lit up with an email from Artemis with the details of the job. He'd never taken a job to kidnap someone, but he knew how it worked. He wasn't surprised to see that the Walker family was ready to pay handsomely to have Cyril taken to them.

He would make sure that never happened.

Vale was still confused by his feelings, but he told himself that he just didn't want an innocent man to suffer needlessly. Cyril hadn't done anything that would warrant anyone hurting him, let alone a crime family. Vale wasn't an angel or a protector, but he was here, and there was no one else to protect Cyril. He could do it until Cyril finally understood what the fuck was happening and made the decision to leave town.

Something told Vale it would take more than a threat in the grocery store parking lot for Cyril to finally understand he couldn't stand up to the Walker family.

Cyril hadn't had a big job for days, and he loved it.

He enjoyed what he did. He had a rare power that people paid handsomely for him to use. He liked not having to worry about how he would pay his bills, and he didn't mind bringing back most of the people he was hired to bring back. He usually tried to look into them before he did so, but unless he found something glaringly bad, like in James Walker's case, usually, he reanimated whoever he was paid to reanimate.

It took a lot out of him, especially when he had to do two

full reanimations so close together, which was why he hadn't taken any jobs lately. No one had called him for a full reanimation, and there were plenty of other necromancers in the city who could take care of shorter reanimations. They wouldn't need a lot of power to ask a dead person a few questions.

So Cyril had been relaxing at home, ordering a lot of takeout, and watching movies and TV series that had been lined up in his to-watch list. He'd also been studying, because as a necromancer, he felt that the more he knew about his art and how it worked, the better it would be. He still hadn't found an explanation for how magic reanimated people, but one day he would. It had to be in a book somewhere.

He was in his kitchen cutting a tomato for a salad when he heard a noise behind him. He turned, a smile on his lips as he expected to find Oscar creeping up behind him to steal a piece of tomato. He screeched when a large figure loomed over him, leaning forward as if to touch him. He acted instinctively, stabbing his knife forward.

The figure jumped back. "Why the fuck are you trying to stab me?" Vale asked.

"Why the fuck are you in my apartment again?" Cyril asked, waving his knife around.

Vale eyed Cyril as if he expected to be stabbed again. Cyril felt guilty because he could see a hole and a bead of blood on Vale's shirt, but Vale shouldn't have snuck up on him, dammit.

The sound of something skittering toward them made Vale jump. He turned toward the door just in time to see Oscar run into the kitchen and launch himself at him. Vale shouted and raised his hands, possibly to push Oscar away, but Oscar wrapped his tentacles around one of Vale's forearms and clung on, even when Vale shook his arm to dislodge him.

Cyril put down his knife and rolled his eyes. Was this

going to happen every time Vale and Oscar were in the same room?

He stepped forward and pried Oscar off Vale's arm. Vale quickly stepped back, still staring at the octopus.

"It attacked me again," he accused.

"Well, that makes sense, since you snuck into my apartment again. What the fuck are you doing here?"

It wasn't that Cyril wasn't happy to see Vale. In a weird way, he was. He didn't have a lot of people in his life. In fact, he only had his mother. Everyone else gave him a wide berth as soon as they found out what he did. Most people disliked dealing with death, let alone seeing it almost every day. Cyril didn't have any friends, because they ran away from him as soon as they found out that he was a necromancer, but Vale knew, and he was still there.

"I need to talk to you," Vale said.

"And you couldn't knock on the door?"

"I wasn't sure you'd open."

"Damn right, I wouldn't have opened. You're an asshole."

"Takes one to know one."

His answer startled Cyril and made him chuckle. "Are we back in school?"

Vale huffed and raked a hand through his hair. "I really need to talk to you, and it's serious."

Cyril wasn't going to like this, was he? "Does it involve the Walker family?"

"It does. They put out a hit on you. They don't want to kill you but to kidnap you, but the result is similar."

"Excuse me? The results of those two actions are *not* similar. They're not trying to kill me, which means I'm not going to be dead by the end of this."

"Being kidnapped by them might be worse. Even if you agree to reanimate James Walker, they won't let you go. You're too precious for them to waste such an opportunity."

Vale was right, even though Cyril didn't want to admit it. He had a hard time believing all of this was real. Just a few weeks ago, his life had been entirely normal—well, normal for him. He'd been reanimating people, reading a lot of old books, and spending time with his mother and Oscar. He wasn't sure he could say he was happy, but he was content, and that was enough for him.

Now he was running from a powerful crime family who wanted him to reanimate their dead boss. He was surprised they hadn't knocked on his door yet, although if he had to guess, he'd say it wouldn't be long before they did. Vale was right. The Walker family would try to take advantage of Cyril now that they knew he existed.

He didn't want to run. This was his home, and he wasn't leaving it. The problem was that he might not have a choice. The Walker family wouldn't take no for an answer, no matter how many times Cyril told them he wouldn't reanimate James Walker. He was making an enemy out of the family, which wasn't a smart thing to do.

What else could he do? He couldn't reanimate James Walker. Cyril had never met the man, but from everything he'd heard, no one deserved to be reanimated less than James Walker. He'd been an abusive bully when he was alive, and that wouldn't change after he was reanimated.

But even if Cyril managed to get out of reanimating James Walker, he wouldn't be out of trouble. The Walker family had set their eyes on him, and they wouldn't let go now that they knew about him. He had to do something, but what?

He was just a necromancer. He didn't know how to deal with crime families or how to defend himself. He'd never had to do any of that.

What the fuck was he going to do?

What was Vale doing? Why had he told Cyril that he was too precious to be hurt?

In a way, he was. With the kind of power Cyril had, he should be protected, not used by an infamous crime family. Vale could too easily imagine what the Walkers would do to Cyril if they got their hands on him, and he wouldn't wish that on his worst enemy, let alone someone as sweet as Cyril.

The problem was that Cyril wasn't just sweet. He was also stubborn as fuck, and Vale wasn't sure how to work around that. Trying to convince Cyril to leave town hadn't worked. What else could he do?

Most people would probably tell him to wash his hands of everything that was happening, but he couldn't. He was in too deep. If he left now, he'd always regret not helping if something happened to Cyril. Besides, it wouldn't be right. Cyril had every right to refuse to work for the Walker family or anyone else. He shouldn't have to pay for that, especially not the way the Walker family would.

He could see Cyril was panicking. His lips were pressed together, his eyes were wide, and his skin had paled. Vale hadn't thought that was possible, because Cyril was already so pale that he looked like his skin never saw the sun, but there he was.

"I know you already said you don't want to do that, but you should leave town for a bit," Vale gently pushed.

Cyril's scowl told Vale that, once again, he wouldn't take his advice. "Why would I let them win?"

"Would you rather have them hurt you? Because that's what will happen if you don't leave."

"I'll find a way to defend myself."

This man was almost as frustrating as Russell. Any kind of conversation with him made Vale want to scream, but he didn't want to freak Cyril out even more, so he sucked in a breath, then another. "You live here. I'm sure you know the

Walker family better than I do, so you have to be aware of what they do. Do you really think people like that will stop trying to get to you just because you don't want to work for them? If you continue being stubborn, they'll either grab you or have someone hurt the people you love. There's already a kidnapping job on your head. They're not doing their dirty work on their own, which means anyone could snatch you off the streets, and no one will know what happened to you. You won't ever see this apartment again." Or his weird ass pet.

"I can't allow them to run me out of my home," Cyril insisted, but his voice had a slight tremble to it. "Yes, I live here. I know what they do, which is why I refused to reanimate James Walker when they asked. I knew it would get me in trouble, but I don't regret doing it. The world is a better place without him, and nothing anyone can do or say will change my mind about that. Besides, I won't have to wait for long. He's already been dead a week. I'm surprised they're still trying to get me to help."

The problem with the fact that Cyril was so sweet was that he didn't understand how criminals thought. "They probably froze his body, but even if they didn't, they can use you in different ways. Once they get their hands on you, you'll be their property."

"No one can own people."

"You think that's going to stop them? They're a crime family. They don't care about laws or how other people feel or think. If they want something, they get it, one way or another, and right now, what they want is you."

Cyril rubbed his face. He was visibly scared, which made Vale regret telling him all of this, but Cyril *needed* to be scared. He needed to realize he was going to get hurt.

"How did you know they were the ones after me, anyway?" Cyril asked. "I never told you about them, yet when you confronted them in the parking lot, you knew who they were."

"Not for sure. I'd heard what happened to James Walker, so it wasn't hard to guess who those guys belonged to. I don't want you to have to belong to the same people."

Cyril stared at Vale. "Why do you care so much? You don't know me. We're not friends. You don't have a reason to protect me or worry about me so much."

Vale wished he had an answer, but even he didn't know why he cared. "You're innocent. I don't often deal with innocent people in my line of work, and I'm not a protector, but this isn't right. The Walker family has no right to do this to you or anyone else, and I feel that someone needs to stop them. Even more so, someone needs to protect you."

"And you'll be the one to do that?"

"You should protect yourself. Leave town, Cyril. Don't make this easy for them."

Cyril was already shaking his head. "I don't have anywhere else to go. I don't *want* to go anywhere else. I'll have to risk it, and hopefully, they'll forget about me after a while. I really don't understand what they would want from me after the body is too degraded to reanimate."

Cyril was too innocent. He couldn't wrap his mind around the fact that someone could keep him prisoner for years, use him when they wanted, and discard him until the next time. He knew how powerful he was, but he couldn't see how that would be useful for a family like the Walkers.

He was also more stubborn than anyone else Vale had ever met. Either that or he was too frightened to move or do anything to protect himself, which was also a possibility. Whatever his reason, it wouldn't change the fact that by staying, Cyril was making himself vulnerable.

"I appreciate that you're trying to help me, but this isn't your business," Cyril said. "You don't have to worry about me, and I don't expect you to protect me."

That wouldn't change the fact that Vale would do precisely that. It might not be his job or his business, but he wouldn't let Cyril get hurt because people felt like they could use and abuse him.

He'd have to watch Cyril from afar and probably ask Russell for help. He wasn't looking forward to that, because his friend would tease him endlessly, but if it meant saving Cyril, he'd do it.

Cyril needed to be saved from the Walker family and from himself, and apparently, Vale would have to be the man for the job. He had no idea when that had happened or why, but he doubted it mattered. The only thing that did was that he would stick around until he could make sure that Cyril was safe.

CHAPTER EIGHT

Cyril stared at the book he was trying to read. He hadn't flipped the page in at least half an hour, if not longer. Instead of reading about reanimation, his every thought had been on Vale.

Not on the Walker family and what they were planning for him. Not on what would happen if they caught him.

On Vale.

This was a disaster. Why was Cyril so obsessed with the man? He could admit that Vale was very good-looking, not beautiful, but handsome. His features were too rugged for him to be beautiful, but Cyril didn't mind, and apparently, neither did his heart.

Or anything lower than his heart.

Now that he wasn't so afraid of Vale, Cyril couldn't stop imagining what might happen between them. He was pretty sure Vale had decided to protect him, since he'd refused again to leave town, which meant he was around here somewhere, watching Cyril.

The thought sent a shiver down Cyril's spine. Thinking of Vale watching him shouldn't be sexy, but it was. It made Cyril want to strip in front of the window and, at the same time check that every single curtain was closed so Vale wouldn't see him without his clothes on.

Cyril wasn't anywhere near as well-built and handsome as Vale. He was short and on the scrawny side. He wouldn't say he was ugly, but beyond his gift of necromancy, he was actually boring. Usually it didn't matter, because being a necromancer meant that people didn't want anything to do with him, but that wasn't the case with Vale. Vale wanted to protect Cyril. He wanted him to be safe. Cyril was still confused by that, because he and Vale weren't friends, and he couldn't imagine Vale doing something like this for someone he disliked.

Or maybe he *would* do this even for people he didn't like. He might be a professional killer, but he seemed to have a personal sense of right and wrong. Cyril had wanted to look into him, but he wouldn't know where to start. He just knew that Vale had killed the last two guys Cyril had fully reanimated but that he didn't want Cyril to be hurt.

Cyril groaned and closed the book after sticking a piece of paper between the pages. He set it down and hugged his knees to his chest, wondering what he was supposed to do.

He didn't feel that important. He understood why the Walker family wanted him, but he doubted he was a priority. They hadn't even tried calling again after what had happened in the parking lot. There was no way they were still after him, was there?

Vale seemed to think they were, and Cyril didn't have the information he did, but it felt too ridiculous.

His phone rang, startling him. He stared at it for a moment as if it might bite him, but he could see his mother's picture on the screen, so he knew it wasn't the Walker family. Since he needed a distraction, he quickly answered. "Hey."

"Weren't we supposed to see each other for coffee this morning?"

Cyril swore and got up from the armchair. "I'm really sorry. I completely forgot."

"You're still at home?"

"Yeah. Give me fifteen minutes, and I'll be there."

"Never mind that. Stay in your apartment. I'll grab coffee and join you so you don't have to come all the way here."

Cyril flopped back. He loved his mom, and in moments like these, he was damn glad to have her. "You're the best mom in the world."

She chuckled. "That's what I think, too. You'll have to tell me why you're so distracted, though. I really hope it's not your job."

Cyril hesitated and instantly knew he'd made a mistake. If it had been the job, he would have told her. He'd never avoided telling her what he was working on and how many jobs he worked. She always said he needed to slow down, but the job was the only thing he had beyond her. He didn't have a social life. He had a few hobbies, but he couldn't stay at home and read the entire day, although it was tempting.

"So it's not the job," she drawled.

Cyril could see her, even though she wasn't in front of him. She no doubt had a smile playing on her lips and a thousand questions already lining up in her mind. She wouldn't hesitate to ask them, either. She wanted to know what Cyril was up to, if he was happy and what was happening in his life. She never pushed, but she also wasn't afraid to ask questions.

Cyril groaned. "It's not the job," he admitted.

Well, not entirely. He was worried about the Walker family, but he still couldn't stop thinking about Vale. Apparently, the man's handsomeness was more important than what might happen to Cyril if the Walker family got their hands on him.

"That sounds like boy trouble."

"I'm not in middle school anymore, Mom. You can't call him a boy." That word just didn't fit Vale.

"Man trouble, then. I didn't know you'd met someone."

"I'm not sure I did."

"But you're thinking about this man. He got you so distracted that you forgot we were supposed to meet for coffee. You know I won't push, but I'm here if you need me."

Cyril sighed. He couldn't tell his mom that he might be in danger, but he could tell her about Vale as long as he changed a few details. "I met him at the grocery store, of all places. He helped me in the parking lot when I dropped my stuff, then offered me coffee. I've only seen him once since then, but he's sweet."

Most people wouldn't think of a professional killer as sweet, but Cyril couldn't help it. Vale *was* sweet. He was so worried about Cyril that it was endearing. Cyril wished he understood the reasons behind Vale's behavior.

"Is he also handsome?"

"Yeah, he is. He's strong and handsome, worries about me, and doesn't seem afraid of me or disgusted by what I do." And that was more unique than rare.

As far as Cyril knew, his mother was the only other person who wasn't frightened by his necromancy. She'd had decades to deal with it, though. She'd known since Cyril was a toddler, but Vale had met Cyril just a few days ago, yet he'd never appeared afraid or wary.

Maybe that was why Cyril was so interested in him. He was the first guy in Cyril's life to seem to like Cyril for who he was. Usually, if Cyril wanted to date, he had to keep the fact that he was a necromancer to himself, but not this time. This time, it was out in the open, and Vale didn't care.

But that didn't mean the two of them would date. Vale was here because he had a job to do, but he'd leave eventually. It would be best if Cyril managed to focus on his work rather than continue obsessing over Vale, but that was easier said than done.

"You can tell me all about him when I get to your apartment."

Cyril's mother sounded excited, probably because she thought like Cyril and that he'd finally found someone. Cyril didn't have it in him to tell her it was all an illusion. Maybe he didn't have to.

He could fake for a little while, then tell her that Vale had left town because he wasn't local. She didn't have to know the details of what was happening between them. She wanted Cyril to be happy and loved. Maybe if they talked about Vale and he embellished the situation a bit, she'd finally be reassured that Cyril would find someone to share his life with.

He wished he could.

Vale should probably yell at Cyril for having all his curtains open, but it made his job easier. It meant he could look right through Cyril's window and see him sitting in his armchair, talking on the phone with someone. Since Cyril was smiling, Vale suspected it wasn't work but a person he cared about, and he was both curious and a bit jealous.

Was it a man? Vale and Cyril weren't dating, and Vale had been careful not to look into Cyril's personal life. It was none of his business, and unlike Cyril's professional life, he didn't need Vale's help with it, so it didn't matter.

What did matter was that Cyril still refused to leave town. Vale had noticed he was being careful now, getting take-out more than he went out for groceries, but that wouldn't help much. Eventually the Walker family would find him, and when they did, they'd grab him.

That was where Vale came in. Right now, he didn't have anything better to do than follow Cyril around and watch him. If the Walker family tried to grab him, Vale would be there to stop them.

Artemis had managed to get the kidnapping job taken down, but Vale was sure another one would come up soon. If it didn't, the Walkers would probably try to get Cyril themselves. Vale might have never worked with them, but he knew the kind of people they were. They felt they were owed everything, and they never hesitated to grab it, even if they had to use violence.

Vale cracked his knuckles. He wanted to use violence against *them*.

"I can't remember the last time I saw you so pissed off," a voice said behind him, making him jump.

He twirled around to glare at Russell, who stood there as if everything was normal.

Russell arched a brow. "I've already been here a few minutes. I might not remember the last time I saw you so pissed off, but I also can't remember the last time I saw you so distracted. What's up with that?"

"What are you doing here?" Vale wasn't going to answer Russell's question. He couldn't admit that Cyril was distracting him.

Russell ignored Vale and moved closer, then peered down.

They were on the roof of the building next to the one where Cyril lived. Luckily, it was summer, so Vale wouldn't have to deal with rain, but it was really fucking hot, and he'd been sweating his ass off. More than once he'd wondered if Cyril would be angry if Vale moved into his apartment with him until this mess was over.

"Oh, I see," Russell said, sounding delighted. "He's really cute. He's the necromancer, right?"

Vale sighed. Once Russell got his claws into something, he didn't let go, not even when it would be better for everyone if he did. No amount of threatening him to stay away would convince him to do so, so Vale might as well pull him in. Besides, he couldn't continue watching Cyril twenty-four-seven. He needed more than cat naps and quick sandwiches to be strong enough to defend Cyril. If he asked Russell for help, he'd be able to rest and eat better, and hopefully, he'd be ready when the Walker family tried something.

He crossed his arms over his chest. "Do you think I would

spy on anyone else?"

"Well, the guy's cute enough for *me* to want to spy on him even though I have no idea who he is, so maybe."

As if Vale would do something like that. He was uneasy enough spying on Cyril as it was. He wouldn't do this to anyone if they weren't in trouble, which was precisely what was happening here.

Vale leaned against the wall. "He's fucking stubborn and won't leave town."

"So you decided to protect him against his will. Well, at least staring at him isn't that bad. He's cute."

"You'll leave him alone. He doesn't need you to make his life messier than it already is."

Russell grinned. "Don't worry. I know you have a crush on him, so I won't try anything."

Vale glared, but deep inside, he couldn't help but wonder if Russell was right.

He thought Cyril was cute. He'd felt that way since the first time he saw him, and there was no reason to deny it. Vale could admit that Cyril was adorable. He made Vale want to wrap him up and hide him from the world, especially since Vale knew in excruciating detail what the world might do to Cyril.

Was that a crush? He didn't know. He didn't have the time to find out, either.

"I just wanted to protect him. He doesn't deserve what the Walker family would do to him if they got their hands on him."

That was enough to make Russell serious. "You're right. No one deserves anything the Walker family would do. They're assholes, and I understand why you want to protect this guy. I'm just not sure you want the attention of the Walker family."

Vale snorted. "I definitely don't, but what choice do I have?

I tried to convince him to leave town, but he won't. He doesn't want to allow them to scare him into running, and while I understand where he's coming from, it's the wrong move."

"That doesn't matter, because you'll protect him. It's why you're here, isn't it? You've been keeping an eye on him because you know the Walker family will eventually try something, and you want to be there to make sure he doesn't get hurt."

Vale turned back to look at Cyril. He wasn't on the phone anymore, and he'd gotten up and was cleaning up his living room. He was also talking, probably to Oscar, which shouldn't be as cute as it was.

"I'll do my best, but I'm only one man."

Russell clasped Vale's shoulder. "No, you're not. I'm here, too, and I'll help you in any way I can."

Vale wasn't surprised. He'd do the same if Russell needed his help. "Thank you."

"You won't be thanking me after I'm done teasing you for having a crush on this guy."

Vale was sure Russell was right, but it didn't matter. Russell was Vale's best friend, and when he needed to be serious, he always was. That was why Vale would trust him with Cyril's life.

But they couldn't do this forever. Eventually, something would break, and Vale prayed that it wouldn't be Cyril.

CHAPTER NINE

Cyril needed more books, which was why he was at the library. Well, that and because he loved the library. Who wouldn't love a place filled with books, especially when they could borrow every single one of them? He didn't want to meet anyone who didn't think libraries were awesome.

His mother was the one who'd started the love of reading in him when he was a child. She enjoyed it as much as he did, although her taste ran more to fiction. Cyril was obsessed with the library's books on necromancy, especially the older ones. He could never afford to buy them for himself, but luckily he didn't have to, because he could borrow them whenever he needed them.

He'd written down several titles of books he needed, so as soon as he reached the library, he went to work. He gathered the books he'd need, but there were more than he could check out, which meant he'd have to take notes before leaving some of them behind. That was fine because the library was full of tables that people used to do homework, study, or just relax.

Cyril chose a table by the window. It was out of the way, surrounded by shelves and stacks of books, so people wouldn't bother him. He'd have enough time to do what he needed before returning the books to their shelves and checking out the others.

He dropped the books onto the table, checked his list again, and realized he'd forgotten one. He left his messenger bag with the pile of books and went in search of the missing book, but he didn't get far.

The guy from the grocery store parking lot, the one who'd smoked, stood in front of him when he turned the corner around a shelf. It was clear he'd been expecting Cyril, but Cyril had no idea how he had found out Cyril would be there.

"Mr. Moreau," the man said.

Cyril scowled at him. "I haven't changed my mind. I'm not reanimating your boss. I don't know who's sending you after me, but you can tell them that."

The man wasn't alone, but Cyril hadn't expected him to be. Two other guys stepped closer. They looked like the ones from the grocery store because they wore similar suits, but he didn't recognize these guys. He knew what they were, though. They were the muscle that would drag Cyril out of the library kicking and screaming if he didn't come along quietly.

He crossed his arms over his chest. He had no intention of doing that. If they even tried to touch him, he'd make a racket loud enough to get everyone running to see what was happening. It was the only way he had to protect himself, and he wasn't afraid of using it.

Besides, he was pretty sure Vale wouldn't allow these guys to hurt him. They hadn't talked again, but Cyril was sure he was watching him. He'd felt it a few times, and once, he'd actually seen Vale skulking around the building next to his.

He really hoped it had been Vale, because if it wasn't, he had a stalker. Cyril already had enough things to worry about without adding a stalker to the mix.

"I understand your reluctance, Mr. Moreau, but I really think you ought to come with us," cigarette-guy said. "You wouldn't want us to start shooting in a library, or maybe to reach out to your mother. She cares very much about you, so I have no doubt that she'd do anything in order to keep you safe."

Cyril swallowed. It was the first time these guys had

threatened his mom, and he didn't like it. He still wouldn't follow them, though. It wouldn't protect his mother. If they wanted to hurt her, they would, whatever Cyril did.

The thought of not giving in was terrifying, but Cyril stood his ground. "Leave my mother alone. She has nothing to do with this."

"Mr. Walker requires your presence at a meeting."

"I really hope that's not James Walker you're talking about," a voice drawled. "Because if it is, things might get awkward. Hasn't he been dead for nearly two weeks by now?"

Cyril didn't recognize the voice, so he wasn't surprised not to recognize the man it belonged to. He stared at him with wide eyes, because while the guy seemed to know who cigarette-man and his goons were, he didn't look afraid.

The man pushed away from the shelf he'd been leaning against and winked at Cyril. He came to stand next to him, slightly ahead of him, as if he wanted to be ready in case these guys tried to grab him.

Cigarette-guy stared at the guy for a moment. "I know you."

The new guy wrinkled his nose. "Unfortunately, you do. I see the Walker family hasn't changed a bit since I last worked for you."

"We haven't requested the help of a professional assassin."

The new guy shrugged. "Then it's a good thing I'm not here for you."

Cigarette-guy looked at Cyril. Cyril had no idea what was happening, but he wasn't about to show it. He wanted cigarette-guy to think this was all planned. Cyril didn't know who this new man was, but he was pretty sure he had to be friends with Vale.

"You shouldn't be involved in this," cigarette-guy said.

"It's a pity I am, then, at least for you. Now, Cyril has work to do, so you better go. I'm sure your boss will want to know what happened today." He grimaced. "I really hope you're not reporting directly to James Walker. That can't be pleasant. Can you imagine the smell?"

Cigarette-guy seemed to weigh his options. He looked around the room, probably thinking he could still try to grab Cyril, but there were too many people there. If the new guy was who Cyril thought he was, he'd be able to protect him, which meant that if cigarette-guy wanted to take Cyril, he'd have to make a mess. He wouldn't be able to do it quietly, because Cyril wouldn't go with him.

"This isn't over," cigarette-guy said as he took a step back. He looked at Cyril. "I hope you know what you're doing, Mr. Moreau. Mr. Walker won't be this nice forever. When he loses his patience, you won't have a choice."

Cyril squared his shoulders. "I'll always have a choice when it comes to using my ability, and I'm not reanimating James Walker, so fuck off and leave me alone."

The new guy snickered. "I already like you," he said.

Since it looked like he'd just saved Cyril, Cyril could say he already liked him, too.

They stood side-by-side as they watched cigarette-guy and the other two men walk out of the library. Cyril only relaxed once the door closed behind them, but he wasn't out of the woods yet.

The new guy turned to him and smiled as he offered his hand. "I'm Russell."

Cyril shook his hand, praying he wasn't making a mistake. "I'm Cyril, and I really hope you're Vale's friend and not a weirdo."

Russell's laughter echoed in the room. "I *really* like you. This is going to be so much fun."

For some reason, those words scared the fuck out of Cyril.

Vale nodded at the woman behind the counter and took the paper bag she was holding out to him. He was tired of sandwiches, but they were the easiest thing to eat while he was following Cyril around town. Things were slightly easier when Cyril was home, but even then, Vale didn't want to leave him on his own for too long. It would be just Vale's luck for the Walker family to try to get to Cyril while he was out somewhere eating lunch.

So once again, sandwiches it was. Vale was pretty sure he wouldn't want to see another piece of bread for a while once this was over.

His phone vibrated in his pocket. He took it out as he left the shop, already worried. He'd left Russell to keep an eye on Cyril, so while he wasn't surprised to see that Russell was calling him, he was annoyed. How was it possible for Russell to be a professional killer when he couldn't even keep an eye on one small necromancer for ten minutes?

"What?" Vale barked out when he answered.

"Who peed in your cereal?"

"What?"

"Never mind. I just wanted to tell you that the Walkers tried to get Cyril, but I kicked them out of the library."

Vale almost dropped the bag of food. "What?" he repeated for the third time.

"It looks like you're getting hard of hearing in your old age. I said that the Walkers tried to get Cyril, but I told them to fuck off. Well, he did, actually. It was pretty funny."

"You weren't supposed to let him see you," Vale said with a growl as he rushed toward the library.

He'd thought Cyril would be safe here for a while, especially with Russell watching him, but he'd been wrong. He was tempted to lock Cyril up in his apartment until he finally agreed to leave town, but he liked his balls attached to his body, and he wouldn't put it past Cyril to try to cut them off if he attempted something like that.

When had Vale's life become so complicated?

"What was I supposed to do? They were going to drag him out of the library. I had to intervene before they could either do that or start shooting, which I'm pretty sure at least one of them was tempted to do. I saw his hand twitch toward his gun."

"Where's Cyril now?"

"Here."

Good Lord. Cyril and Russel were together? As in, they were spending time together, probably talking about Vale, and who knew what else? This sounded like a disaster in the making, and Vale had to get to the library before something else happened. "I'll be there in five minutes."

"No rush. Cyril's safe, and he seems to like me."

They really were getting to know each other. This wasn't what Vale had in mind when he'd asked Russell to keep an eye on Cyril. They weren't supposed to make friends. Russell was there to keep an eye on Cyril, but Vale should have known something would go wrong.

He rushed back to the library, wondering what he'd find when he got there. There were no signs of anyone from the Walker family, but he was still careful as he walked in and looked around. Cyril had chosen a table under a window tucked behind the tall bookshelves, and Vale went straight there, still glancing around, just in case.

He heard the laughter before he could see the table, but he knew who it was. He'd heard Russell laugh hundreds of times over the years they'd known each other. When Russell worked, he was serious, but that was the only part of his life he took that way. The rest of the time, he always had a smile on his lips.

Vale stepped around the shelf and stared. Cyril and Russell

were both seated at the table. The pile of books next to him appeared unread, and he didn't look interested in any of the books. Instead, his attention was on Russell, who was sitting in front of him. Russell's feet were on the table, and he'd tilted his chair on its back legs. If he wasn't careful, he'd fall back and hurt his head, but he'd always had phenomenal balance.

Russell's head was thrown back as he laughed. Vale noticed a few people looking around, probably to find him. He doubted they'd reprimand him for laughing in the library. People usually loved Russell's laugh. Hell, people usually loved *Russell*. He was always happy, talked to pretty much anyone without hesitation, and was always willing to help people. It was why he was here. He wanted to help Vale, and after he'd found out about Cyril, he'd been curious.

It looked like he wouldn't have to be curious for much longer, since the two of them seemed to have become best friends over the past ten minutes.

Vale rushed to Cyril, who looked up as he reached him. His eyes widened when Vale dropped his bag onto the table and cupped his cheek with one hand. Vale startled himself with the gesture, but he was too far gone to stop.

He gently turned Cyril's head this way and that. "Are you all right? Did they hurt you? What happened?"

Cyril wrapped his fingers around Vale's wrist. For a moment, Vale thought he would push him away, but instead, he squeezed. He didn't let go even as he smiled.

"I'm fine. Russell stepped in before they could do anything." He swallowed and looked around. "I don't think they're here anymore, but they threatened my mother."

Vale wasn't surprised. Actually, he was surprised they'd waited so long. Cyril didn't seem to be afraid for himself, so it made sense to go for the person he *would* be afraid for. From what Vale had seen, there weren't many people in Cyril's life, but he was close to his mother, so it was a good guess that he might do what they wanted if they threatened her.

"I won't let anything happen to her, either," Vale promised.

Cyril nodded. "I knew they'd hurt her even if I said yes to whatever they want from me, so I told them to leave."

"You did the right thing. I'm sorry I wasn't there for you. I should have been."

"What am I, chopped liver?" Russell grumbled.

Cyril smiled and let go of Vale's wrist. It was ridiculous for Vale to continue holding onto him like this, so he let go, even though he didn't want to.

What the fuck was happening to him?

Vale turned to glare at his friend. "You're not, but I told you to watch Cyril from afar, not to ride in on your white horse and save him from the Walker family."

"What was I supposed to do?" Russell asked as he straightened his chair. "Let them drag him out?"

Vale rubbed his face. "No. You did the right thing." But he'd attracted the attention of the Walker family. They knew Cyril was protected by Russell and Vale now. Vale had no idea how they'd react to it, but he wasn't looking forward to finding out.

"You were right," Cyril murmured. "I should have listened to you and left town, but I still don't want to. I also don't want to continue hiding, though." He looked at Vale. "What can I do? Can I hire you?"

Vale stared. "For what?" he croaked.

"To get rid of whoever's coming after me."

Those were the last words Vale expected to hear coming from Cyril's mouth. "You're not the kind of person who hires people like me or Russell."

"Maybe not, but I feel I should. They threatened my mother."

Vale wasn't surprised that Cyril was willing to hire a

professional killer to protect his mother but hadn't thought about doing it to protect himself. "That's a last resort, okay? We should talk and sort out the situation. Once we have all the information down, we can make decisions."

Vale might not know Cyril very well, but he could tell that Cyril would regret it if he tried to hire him. Cyril wasn't the kind of person who killed or had others killed easily. Even though the Walker family was dangerous and had made an enemy out of Cyril, he wouldn't send professional killers after them. He didn't have it in him, which was one of the reasons Vale liked him so much.

Russell got to his feet. "Well, I'm headed out. Let me know what you decide." He winked at Cyril. "You have my number now, cutie. Use it if you need it."

Vale pressed his lips together and told himself that this was none of his business. If Russell and Cyril wanted to start dating, he didn't have anything to say about it.

Really.

Cyril watched Russell walk away. He'd been surprised when he'd realized that Vale wasn't watching him, but since he could smell the food in the bag Vale had been carrying, he understood why. Russell had assured him that Vale had to step away for a moment, and he'd been right. Vale had needed to eat.

Cyril started gathering his notebook and the books he'd be checking out. He'd have to come back to take notes from the others, but that was all right. Right now, he wanted to leave the library and not think about what had happened earlier for a while. He was pretty sure he wouldn't get to do that, but at the very least, he could give Vale the opportunity to eat. He was kind of hungry himself, now that he thought about it.

"What are you doing?" Vale asked as he watched Cyril.

"Packing up. You need to eat, and you can't do that here. Besides, I don't think I can focus on any of these books today."

"I'm sorry I wasn't here to protect you."

Cyril stopped moving and looked around. They were alone, although he could hear a few people talking between the shelves. Still, the privacy was enough that he allowed himself to answer. "You have nothing to be sorry about. I'm not paying you to protect me, and Russell was there. I was safe."

"You don't even know Russell."

"But I was sure he was there because of you. You wouldn't leave me on my own."

Which was a problem. Vale looked exhausted, and Cyril wondered when he'd last slept a full eight hours. Was he watching Cyril even during the night? That was when Cyril was more vulnerable, and while he didn't mind the thought of Vale watching him, he disliked thinking of him sleeping on the roof — if he slept at all.

"It won't happen again," Vale promised.

"You can't watch me twenty-four hours a day, seven days a week. You're human. Maybe we can find a way to keep me protected when you need to sleep or step away." Cyril's mind went straight to a small skeleton army. He would never dare use his power that way in the city, where anyone could see it, but if it was necessary, he might ignore his own arguments against creating it.

This was a necromancer's power, too. He could reanimate dead bodies, whatever state they were in. He could even cobble together bones and create new bodies, like he had with Oscar. It wasn't a power many necromancers used because it would be useless to reanimate a skeleton, but they could do it.

Cyril tried to imagine having an army of skeletons ready to defend him. He was pretty sure the Walker family would run away screaming bloody murder, which meant he was tempted to create the army just to see that.

"You're planning something I'm not going to like," Vale drawled.

Cyril blinked up at him. "What are you talking about?"

To his surprise, Vale reached out and bopped him on the nose. They stared at each other for a few seconds, and Cyril was delighted to see Vale's cheeks turn pink.

"I recognize that expression," Vale said after clearing his throat. "It means mischief."

"I was just trying to think about some way I could protect myself using my power. Maybe I could create an army of Oscars."

Vale shuddered with what Cyril knew was horror. For some reason, Vale didn't find Oscar as adorable as Cyril did.

"Please, no. I'll protect you, but don't even think about creating more of those things," Vale said.

Cyril was all packed up, so Vale picked up his bag. Cyril's stomach growled at the thought of the food inside of it, which earned him an amused glance from Vale. He followed Cyril to the front desk so that he could register the books he was checking out before they left the library.

"You should get something to eat," Vale said once they were outside.

"So should you. I also think you need to get some sleep before you fall on your face while you're trying to fight the Walker family. You wouldn't want to let them win just because you're exhausted, would you?"

Thankfully, Vale didn't seem to mind that Cyril was being rude. If anything, he was clearly amused. "Is that your way of telling me I look like shit?"

Cyril laughed. "A bit. It's obvious you're not sleeping well." He hesitated. He couldn't believe he was about to make this offer, but it was the only thing that made sense. "I know you've been watching me from the roof of the building next to mine. You're probably doing it at night, too, and I was wondering if it wouldn't be easier for you to move into my apartment with me for a bit."

Cyril felt safer knowing that Vale was watching him, but he didn't want Vale to suffer because of his problems. Vale didn't need to be that close to protect him, but it would make things easier for both of them.

It would also make things more awkward. Cyril wasn't sure how he felt about Vale. He liked the man, and he wasn't wary of him anymore. He also wasn't afraid, even though he knew what kind of job Vale did for a living. They hadn't spent a lot of time together, but Cyril enjoyed their banter. He didn't want Vale to get hurt protecting him, but he also didn't want to be kidnapped and forced into submission by the Walker family.

"Well, it would make things easier," Vale said.

"I know I'm being difficult and that it would be even easier if I agreed to leave town, but I'm scared that if I do that, I won't ever be able to come back. I don't want to hide for the rest of my life or to have to leave my home."

Because Vale was right. Even if the Walker family couldn't force Cyril to reanimate James Walker before his body degraded too much, they could use him for other things. They could continue threatening him and his mother every time they wanted something and he dared to say no. That wasn't the kind of life he wanted, but he didn't know what to do. If he continued saying no, the family would hurt him and his mother. If he said yes, they would force him to do things he would never want to do for them or anyone else. There wasn't a way for him to win this, but he was grateful for Vale's presence. Knowing he was there had made Cyril's life easier, but clearly, the same couldn't be said for Vale.

Cyril didn't understand why Vale and Russell were

helping him, but he was done protesting. It looked like whatever he said, they wouldn't change their minds about it, so he might as well take advantage of it. He'd hoped the Walker family would realize he was protected and would leave him alone, but he was starting to doubt that. Still, he didn't want to make Vale's job harder.

"I understand your reaction," Vale said in a soft voice. "I don't blame you for not wanting to leave. Russell and I will do everything we can to keep you safe, so I don't want you to worry about what will happen to you or your mother."

Cyril nodded. "All right. I'm still going to tell her to go on vacation."

"That's probably a good idea. The Walkers wouldn't hesitate to use her to force you into things. They haven't been able to convince you, and she's the only person you care about."

That had been true once, but Cyril was starting to wonder if it still was because when he looked at Vale, he felt like he cared. At the very least, he didn't want Vale to be hurt, and he definitely didn't want him to leave.

What did that mean?

It was clear that Cyril had been spooked by what had happened at the library even after they stopped to eat lunch. He was more pliant than before, and while Vale wouldn't be able to convince him to leave town, he had at least agreed to be more careful. Sending his mother out of the city was also a good idea, and it was a relief to know that Vale wouldn't have to protect her, too. He would have if he had to, but he'd rather focus on keeping Cyril safe.

Vale parked behind Cyril's building in case they needed to make a quick escape, then rushed over to help him as he stepped out of his car. Cyril balanced the books he'd borrowed from the library in his arms, and when the top of the pile started to slide, Vale snatched them from his arms before they could fall. Cyril gave him a grateful smile, then gestured toward the front door.

"I guess you already know where I live, so I don't have to invite you up."

"I don't have to stay with you if you're uncomfortable with it," Vale reassured him.

"I'm more uncomfortable with what the Walker family is doing. It's just going to be odd, because I've been living on my own for a while now."

Vale could understand that. He'd lived alone since he was seventeen, starting on the streets. Now, he had his own apartment, but he didn't spend a lot of time there. The place was anonymous, unlike Cyril's place.

Vale looked around as they walked in. He'd watched Cyril unlock the door, so he knew it hadn't been open, but he wouldn't put it past the Walkers to find a way inside.

Vale set down the books and went through the apartment, keeping an eye and an ear open. It looked like they were alone, though, and when he returned to Cyril, it was to find him making tea.

"Do you want one?" Cyril asked.

"Please, and thank you."

Cyril gestured at Vale to sit at the small table in the kitchen. Vale obeyed and watched him until he heard the characteristic sound of Oscar coming closer. He winced, unable to stop himself. The sound of Oscar's bones clacking on the floor made Vale shudder in horror.

"You really don't like Oscar," Cyril said as he sat on the other chair after placing two mugs on the table.

"It's not that I don't like him. It's just weird."

Cyril looked a little sad as he leaned down and picked up Oscar. Vale did his best not to wince at the sight of the bone tentacles, but it wasn't easy. Cyril didn't seem to have a problem with Oscar. He stroked the skull, looking like he was cuddling a cat.

"I was lonely when I created him. I still am sometimes, but I've made my peace with the fact that most people want nothing to do with me."

"Because you're a necromancer?"

Cyril nodded. "I understand why they feel that way. Death is something most people don't want to deal with, and I don't blame them for that. I just wish they could see beyond me being a necromancer."

The sadness in his voice made Vale want to find every single person who'd ever rejected him and beat them to a pulp. Since he couldn't do that, he reached out and gently touched Cyril's hand. Cyril turned wide eyes to him, and Vale couldn't stop himself.

He leaned forward, gently pressing their lips together. Cyril sucked in a breath, and even though Vale wanted to deepen the kiss, he didn't. He pressed their lips together again, then leaned back and smiled at Cyril.

"It sounds like you met a lot of assholes. I have, too, but not everyone is like that. There are people in the world who won't care that you're a necromancer."

"Like you?"

There was so much hope in Cyril's voice that Vale couldn't have said no even if he'd wanted to.

He didn't want to. This didn't feel like something he'd normally do, but he'd reached a point where he didn't care. He wanted to protect Cyril and give him everything he would ever ask for. It wasn't just that Cyril was cute. From what Vale had seen, he was a good person who tried to do the right thing. He'd noticed that Cyril didn't just work for wealthy people. Over the past few weeks, he'd taken several jobs from people who couldn't afford full reanimations, and a few times, he'd refused any payment.

He wanted to help people. He also had to make a living, which was probably why he did reanimations for rich clients, but it was clear his heart was set on helping the people who didn't have a lot. He wanted them to be soothed by his ability to bring back their loved ones for a little while so they could say goodbye.

Cyril was a lovely man, and he didn't deserve what the Walker family was doing to him. Vale would ensure they never hurt him, and if it was in his power, he also wanted to make Cyril happy. This might be nothing like his usual behavior, but at this point, he didn't think it mattered. He wanted Cyril, and he was pretty sure that Cyril wanted him.

Vale would find out, but first, he had to make sure Cyril was safe.

CHAPTER TEN

"As far as I can see, beyond killing half of the Walker family, I don't see how we can convince them to leave Cyril alone," Artemis said.

Vale was sitting on Cyril's couch. Cyril was in the kitchen, humming as he cooked, which had given Vale the opportunity to call Artemis and find out what she was up to. He'd asked her to look into the Walker family and try to find a way to get them off Cyril's back, but she didn't have good news.

"What about Russell?" he asked. "Have you heard from him?"

"I called to ask him about the family, and he told me everything he knew, but there wasn't much I wasn't already aware of. James Walker was an asshole, and it looks like his son isn't far behind. He's already ruling the family with an iron fist."

Vale frowned. "Why would he want his father to be reanimated, then? Wouldn't he want to stay in charge?"

"Well, I'm not in his head, but maybe he loved his father."

Vale almost dismissed that right away, but Artemis might not be wrong. No matter how cruel these people were, they had familial bonds. Paul Walker had grown up with his father. He'd been a child who'd loved his dad, and while Vale had no way of knowing how Paul Walker felt about his father now, he wanted him back for a reason. If it was only to say goodbye or to get information, he wouldn't have to have his father reanimated permanently, so there had to be more. Vale couldn't think of anything beyond Paul Walker loving his father and missing him.

That didn't match with what he knew about the Walker family, but maybe it didn't have to. Vale didn't need to know why these people were doing this. He just had to know that they were and that he needed to protect Cyril. It would be easier if he knew what he was protecting him from, but he could work with this, too.

"I'm really sorry," Artemis said. "I want to protect Cyril as much as you do, but I don't see what we can do about this beyond eliminating the entire family."

And that would take more than just Russell and Vale.

The sound of skittering made Vale shiver, but he stayed where he was. He'd been giving Oscar a wide berth since he'd moved in with Cyril, but for some reason, the weird pet seemed to love Vale. Now that he'd gotten over his mistrust of him, he wouldn't leave him alone. Vale found him everywhere he went in the apartment, including sitting on the coffee table, staring at him while he slept.

That had been a shitty way to wake up.

A white tentacle appeared at the edge of the couch, then another. Oscar hauled himself up onto the cushion, then hesitated. Vale had been watching Cyril, so he knew that Oscar enjoyed being petted while he slept in Cyril's lap. Was that what he wanted from Vale? Vale couldn't think of anything worse, but he really liked Cyril, and Cyril was a package deal with Oscar. That meant that if Vale wanted to be in Cyril's life, he'd have to take Oscar, too.

Vale *did* want to be in Cyril's life, but he couldn't imagine what that would look like. There was too much to do first, too many things to worry about. He didn't even live in the same city, but thankfully, it wouldn't be hard for him to move. There was nothing much in his apartment. The only reason he lived there was that at the time, he'd had to choose a place, and Boston had been the closest city to where he was. Russell had moved there for a few years, too, but he never stayed still for long, so Vale was alone in the city.

He wouldn't be alone if he moved closer to Cyril.

It was way too soon to think about that. Cyril would see it as a huge commitment. He probably wouldn't understand that this city was the same as any other to Vale.

Except that wasn't quite true. Vale wanted to be where his people were, and he only had three of them. Rachel and Russell were often on the move, but Cyril wasn't. He was firm that he wanted to stay here, which made the city all that more appealing for Vale.

"Let me know if you find out anything," he told Artemis.

"I promise I will. We both know that the Walker family isn't going to let this go. They want Cyril, and they've never hesitated to hurt, torture, and kill to get what they want. If it was someone else, I'd ask you if you were sure you wanted to stand with Cyril, but I won't even try."

Oscar inched closer to Vale. When Vale looked at him, he turned his head the other way, acting like nothing was up. It was fucking creepy because Oscar was a skull, but it had become easier to look at him without wanting to run away screaming.

"I'd be the first out of town if Cyril agreed to it," Vale told Artemis as he kept an eye on Oscar.

The bony octopus inched closer again. When Vale didn't turn to look at him, he slid all the way up to him and climbed onto his lap. Even though Vale had expected it, he still had to fight the urge to throw Oscar on the other side of the room. He didn't know if Oscar would feel pain, and he wasn't about to try and find out.

Oscar made a weird purring sound as he folded his tentacles under himself and settled into Vale's lap. He was almost like a cat—if a cat was made of hard bones and two bottomless eye sockets.

Oscar seemed happy, but Vale tentatively raised a hand and stroked his fingers on top of his head. It was weird as fuck to be stroking bone, but Oscar made the purring sound again as if he enjoyed it.

"Is that a cat?" Artemis asked.

Vale wasn't about to tell her and Russell about Oscar. They'd be here to check out the pet within seconds, and Vale didn't want to deal with all the questions. "It's Cyril's pet. Keep me updated, all right? I know Russell decided to stay around until this mess was over, but I'm not sure I can ask him to continue doing so when there's no end in sight."

"As if telling him you're fine on your own will do anything. You know he'll stick with you until this is over, and maybe even after that. He's been talking about settling down."

Vale snorted. "No one believes he wants to settle down. He loves his freedom too much."

"I don't know. He certainly loved it before, but always being on the move becomes old really fast, Vale. You don't realize it because you don't move around as much as we do, but sometimes, I dream of being able to stop."

Vale's chest felt tight. "Maybe it's time for all three of us to retire."

"Maybe. I don't know what I'd do if I didn't have work, though."

And it was too dangerous for her to stay in the same place if she continued being a handler. The three of them had big decisions to make, but Vale wouldn't do anything until he was sure Cyril was safe. Maybe once he was, he and Cyril could talk and find out if they both wanted the same thing. Vale hadn't expected to start his retirement with a relationship, but he wasn't opposed to it. It was one of the reasons he'd been thinking about retiring.

His life had never been normal. He'd been kicked out as a teenager when he'd come out to his parents, but even before then, they'd never been a loving kind of family. After he'd left home, he'd been on his own for a while, then his mentor had found him. He'd never really made friends beyond Russell and Rachel. He'd had plenty of people to fuck, but never a relationship. At almost forty, it was kind of sad.

It was time to get rid of the Walker family. For the first time, Vale was eager to see what the future held, but he wouldn't be able to until the Walker family was out of his life.

And maybe out of the city entirely.

Cyril could hear that Vale was on the phone. He didn't know with whom, but he was curious, and since he was pretty sure Vale was talking about him, he figured it wouldn't be a problem if he listened in for a bit. He'd put the chicken in the oven and had cleaned up, so the only thing he needed to do now was wait, which left him at a loss. Normally, he'd go to the living room and grab a book, maybe put something on TV, but Vale had settled on the couch. The last thing Cyril wanted to do was bother him, but he poked his head out of the kitchen to check in on him.

From where he was, Cyril could see the couch from the side. Vale had settled in what was Oscar's spot on the couch. That was why Cyril wasn't surprised to find his pet in Vale's lap. If Oscar couldn't get to the couch, he just sat on top of whatever was on it.

What Cyril *was* surprised about was that Vale wasn't screaming or pushing Oscar away. He was still talking on the phone, and while he did so, he'd started idly stroking the top of Oscar's head. Even from where Cyril was, he could hear Oscar's weird purr of pleasure.

He still wasn't sure how Oscar could do that. One of the bones he'd used for Oscar's tentacles had probably belonged to a cat, but Cyril couldn't remember. It didn't matter, anyway. What *did* matter was that Vale seemed to have accepted Oscar, which pleased Cyril. He had no idea what he and Vale were doing, but he didn't want to have to choose between Vale and Oscar. He understood why Vale was creeped out by Oscar, but he was sure Vale would get used to Oscar eventually.

A knock on the door made him frown as he turned. He wasn't expecting visitors, but it wouldn't be the first time his mother visited without calling him first. He'd tried to get her to stop doing it, but so far, he hadn't managed.

He moved toward the door to open it, but before he could reach it, Vale was there. His expression was serious as he shook his head, gently pushing Cyril toward the kitchen. "I'll open the door."

"It's probably my mother."

"It could be someone else. Let me take care of this, all right?"

Cyril swallowed. He hadn't even thought that it could be the Walker family. It seemed odd for them to knock on his door, but he supposed anything was possible.

He nodded and watched Vale move closer to the door. There was another knock, and Vale carefully opened. For a few seconds, Cyril held his breath. When Vale opened the door wider, Cyril relaxed.

Unfortunately, that only lasted for a few seconds.

"I don't know you," Cyril's mother told Vale. "Who are you? Where's my son?"

"I'm here," Cyril said as he rushed forward.

He stumbled on a shoe he'd left there and almost fell, catching himself on Vale's shoulder. Vale rolled his eyes and helped him regain his footing, and by the time Cyril looked at his mother, her eyes were gleaming. The fact that Vale's hand was still on Cyril's waist probably had a lot to do with that.

"I wasn't expecting you," he told his mother as he waved

at her to come in.

"I can see that," she answered. She looked Vale up and down.

"This is Vale."

Cyril's mom offered Vale her hand. He shook it without hesitation, even smiling a bit.

"I'm Eva, Cyril's mother," she explained. "And who are you, Vale?"

"He's my boyfriend," Cyril blurted out.

He didn't know if he and Vale were boyfriends. They'd kissed, and Cyril definitely wanted them to be boyfriends, but he wouldn't push Vale into something he didn't want. They needed to talk about it, but now clearly wasn't the right moment. Cyril probably shouldn't have told his mother he and Vale were together, but it was too late, and there was no taking back the words.

She looked pleased as she watched Vale. "Your boyfriend? I didn't know you had a boyfriend."

"It's new," Cyril explained. "We met recently and have been getting to know each other. I didn't tell you because I wasn't sure where it was going."

Vale smiled easily and wrapped an arm around Cyril's shoulders. "But I couldn't resist your son, so here we are."

Cyril's mother was watching them. She'd probably be able to tell if they were lying, but they weren't, not quite. Hopefully, that would be enough to fool her. Cyril really didn't want to have to explain that Vale was a professional killer who was currently protecting him from the Walker family. He'd tried to convince his mother to go on a vacation, but without being able to explain why he wanted her to leave town, he hadn't managed. He still hoped she might listen to him, but now that she knew he had a boyfriend, there would be no traveling for her.

"I can go," she offered. "I didn't mean to bother you. I just wanted to check in on Cyril."

"You should stay for dinner," Vale offered. "Cyril was cooking for us, and while I'm not sure about the quantity of food he cooked, we can find something for everyone to eat or order take-out."

Cyril's mother appeared pleased. She'd probably expected Vale to be eager to get her out of the apartment, but he seemed comfortable with her there. He didn't seem to care that they'd gone from their first kiss to him meeting Cyril's mother in just a few days.

"That sounds nice," Cyril's mother said. "As long as I'm not bothering you." She looked at Cyril, who shook his head.

"It's fine. There's enough food for you, too."

He wanted to check on the chicken, but he was afraid to leave his mother alone with Vale. He didn't think Vale would explain to her why he was really there or what was happening with the Walker family, but he knew his mother well. She would ask all sorts of questions she shouldn't be asking, from what Vale did for a living to how old he was.

The problem was that he would have to leave them alone eventually. The chicken was calling his name from the oven, and it wouldn't be long before it was ready.

To Cyril's shock, Vale kissed the top of his head. "You don't have to stay with us if you need to go back to the kitchen. I don't think your mother's going to eat me. I could help with the food, though."

Vale had been affectionate when it was only the two of them, but this was new. Cyril hadn't expected Vale to be like this, even in front of his mom.

It was the first time he introduced a boyfriend to his mother. The few times he'd managed to hang on to someone for a bit, they'd been uncomfortable with the thought of meeting his mom. That was understandable, but it meant that Cyril had no idea what he was doing today.

He looked from his mother to Vale. He supposed he was going to have to trust them.

Vale was amused. It was clear that Cyril didn't want to leave him and his mother alone, and Vale suspected he knew why. Eva was staring at him, clearly ready to ask him a bunch of questions as soon as Cyril left them.

Vale had never gone through the meeting-the-parents thing. He'd never had a serious relationship that would warrant it, which was just as well. He felt a bit awkward, but it was nothing he couldn't deal with, especially if it was for Cyril.

Cyril looked from his mother to Vale again. He nodded and stepped toward the kitchen, so Vale turned his attention to Eva, smiling at her. "Why don't we sit on the couch?"

"Of course. Cyril, you're sure you don't need any help in the kitchen?"

"I'm fine," Cyril promised. "Be nice, all right?"

His mother chuckled. "When have I ever not been nice?"

Cyril looked like he had an answer to that question but didn't dare say it. Eventually, he retreated to the kitchen, but Vale could tell he wouldn't leave them alone for long.

Oscar had settled back onto the couch after Vale had gotten up. Since there was another spot on the couch and two empty armchairs, Vale sat in one of those while Eva chose the couch. She rubbed her fingertips on top of Oscar's head, but her attention was entirely on Vale.

"You're older."

Vale wasn't surprised that that was what she started with. "I am. I'll turn forty next year."

Eva appeared to be in her sixties, which wasn't surprising since Cyril was in his late twenties. She wore a pale yellow dress and sandals, and her graying dark hair was braided and hung over one shoulder. She wore big hoop hearings and a little makeup, and her skin was slightly pink, as if she hadn't used enough sunscreen. Cyril was as pale as she was, and they looked like each other. Their eyes held the same intelligence, and Vale knew he'd have to be careful. He didn't want Eva to find out what he did for a living and freak out.

"Cyril isn't thirty yet," she commented.

"I'm aware. He doesn't have a problem with the age difference, though, and neither do I."

"Oh, I don't care about the age difference. I just care that you treat my son right." She glanced toward the kitchen. "He's been disappointed often enough. I don't want him to have to go through that again. I'm not asking what your intentions are, but I want you to know that if you hurt him, I'll hunt you down and kill you so badly that he won't be able to reanimate you."

Vale snorted. "I don't think he'd be happy if he had to reanimate me."

"I don't care. Cyril is precious and too sweet for this world. It might not be my job to protect him anymore, but it doesn't mean I'm not going to. Has he told you about the other people in his life?"

"I know he doesn't have many. Most are afraid of him because of what he can do."

Eva nodded. "He got that from his father. When I realized what he could do when he was two, I freaked out. I knew how hard his life would be because of it, and I didn't know how to deal with it. He grew up to be a wonderful man, but his heart has been battered and bruised. He's lonely, not because he wants to be, but because he's forced to be. People don't understand him and think he's a monster just because of what he can do, and that's not fair."

Vale agreed. He wasn't offended by the way Eva was protecting her son. If anything, he was glad that Cyril had her.

She clearly loved her son, which was enough for Vale.

"I can't promise everything will always go smoothly between us or that we won't ever break up, but I like Cyril. I like him enough that I'm planning to move here from Boston."

Eve's eyes widened a bit. "Really?"

"I work for the government." It was the excuse Vale always used to explain his job. People could understand it better than him killing people for money. "I can't talk about it, but it's not an easy job, and I was ready for retirement before I met Cyril. I've been working toward it for the past few years, but I didn't know what I would do with my life once I stopped working. Then I met Cyril, and I'm even more eager to retire."

"You don't care that he's a necromancer?"

"I do, because I think it made him the man he is. Your son is an extremely caring man, Eva. He's sweet and gentle, and I've seen him with the people he works for. He wants to help everyone. He doesn't want people to have to give up saying goodbye to someone they love just because they can't afford to pay him. Not many people would do something like that, but he does. He uses his ability to help people, and that's commendable."

"Dinner is ready," Cyril called out.

Vale and Eva stared at each other for a moment. Vale hadn't meant to say those things, but he wanted Eva to understand that he wouldn't abandon Cyril. He might not be able to promise he'd always be there for him, especially considering his line of work, but he wasn't going anywhere as long as he had a choice and Cyril wanted him.

Eva got to her feet. "That's good to hear. My son deserves to be happy, and if you make him happy, I don't have anything to say about you or your relationship with Cyril. I just wanted you to be aware of what he's been through."

"He mentioned it. I'm not surprised people tend to avoid him, although if I could, I'd have a few words with them."

Eva snickered. "I'd pay to see that."

They joined Cyril in the kitchen. Vale could see he was worried from the way he stared at Vale and Eva, so he quickly wrapped an arm around his shoulders and kissed his cheek. Cyril's skin flushed, but he looked pleased, and when he glanced up at Vale, Vale smiled at him.

"You can stop worrying," Eva said as she sat at the table. "I approve."

"You do?"

"Yes, even though I realize that you don't need my approval to be with him or anyone else. I think you found a good one, though."

Cyril glanced up at Vale again. "I did," he murmured.

As they sat down for dinner, Vale was happy to lean back and let Eva and Cyril carry on the conversation. He thought the evening went well, and he liked Eva, but he was relieved when she finally left about an hour after dinner was over. She had plans for the rest of the evening.

So did Vale.

"Thank you for not telling her I was lying when I said you were my boyfriend," Cyril murmured as they sat on the couch after cleaning up the kitchen. "I panicked. I could have told her you were a friend, but I don't think she would have believed me."

"Why wouldn't she have?" Vale asked, even though he already knew the answer.

Cyril's cheeks flushed pink. "She would have seen how I look at you."

No one should be so adorable. Cyril was a powerful necromancer, yet here he was, blushing and bouncing his knee. Vale didn't want him to be uncomfortable, but after everything that had happened, he wanted things to be clear between them.

"I don't think you were lying to your mother."

Cyril frowned. "What do you mean?"

"I did kiss you. We haven't talked about it, but I wouldn't mind being your real boyfriend." He didn't want Cyril to have to lie to his mother, but more importantly, he wanted them to be together.

He had no idea what he was doing when it came to relationships, but the same went for Cyril, so hopefully, they could muddle their way through this together.

Vale had to be teasing. Cyril tried to read his expression to make sure, but he couldn't. They didn't know each other well, and more than that, Vale's job meant that he was a pro at not showing people how he felt.

Cyril didn't like that, but it wasn't his place to say anything about it. He forced a smile on his lips, convinced as he was that Vale was just joking around. "I'm sure there are better people than me you'd want to be saddled with."

Vale's expression stayed serious. He never once looked away from Cyril, which made Cyril squirm a bit. He wasn't used to people staring at him like that, especially when there was no disgust or fear in their expression.

"There aren't. I've had plenty of opportunity to choose someone else, but I was never interested."

"And you're interested in *me*?"

Vale finally smiled. He took Cyril's hand, which left Cyril unsure what to do. Had he ever held hands with anyone before? He didn't think so. He didn't like lying to people, so when they appeared interested in him, he was honest and told them that he was a necromancer. He wanted them to know before they got in too deep, and the result was always that they dumped him as fast as they could and never looked back. It was either that or just sex, which Cyril had done a few times, but it wasn't satisfying. No, Cyril wanted someone who would see him and love him even though he was a nec-romancer, and he was starting to wonder if maybe he'd found that someone.

It was hard to believe, but there was no denying the way Vale was looking at Cyril. He wasn't rushing to get out of the apartment now that Cyril's mother had left. He hadn't seemed intimidated by her or by the fact that she thought he and Cyril were together. He'd stuck around, talked to Cyril's mother, and acted as if he and Cyril were boyfriends.

And now, he was asking Cyril if he wanted to be his *real* boyfriend.

"I'm more than a little interested in you," Vale said. "I thought it was obvious, but clearly, I need to say the words."

"I'm not sure I can believe you even if you say them."

That wiped the smile off Vale's face. Cyril wanted to bring it back, but he didn't know how or even why it had disappeared.

"I don't know how people have treated you before, but I can imagine it wasn't well. If I could, I'd beat all of them up for being assholes to one of the sweetest men I've ever met," Vale said.

"Me?"

"No, Oscar. Yes, of course you, Cyril. You're sweet and much nicer than most people deserve, and if you'll have me, I want us to be together."

Cyril's mouth was dry. "Of course I'll have you." How could he say no?

"Is it only because you think you can't have anyone else?"

Cyril suddenly realized that he wasn't the only one who was unsure of himself. He was used to rejection and always expected it, but he couldn't imagine that having a relationship had been any easier for Vale. He had to either hide what he did for a living or be honest and watch the person he wanted run from him or, worse, call the cops on him. Cyril could only imagine how careful Vale had to have been in previous relationships and how taxing that would have been on him.

But Cyril already knew what Vale did. They were well-suited—Vale killed people while Cyril reanimated them.

He leaned sideways and kissed Vale. "I would choose you even if half the city wanted to be with me."

That put the smile right back on Vale's face, which thrilled Cyril. He'd been one who made this man smile. He wanted to make Vale happy and had every intention of learning how to do that.

"Good," Vale said. "Because I want you. I don't know how you managed, but you got under my skin in just a few weeks. I can't imagine not being here with you."

"How's that going to work? You don't live in the city, do you?"

Vale shrugged. "That's easily fixed. I'll sell my apartment and move closer to you."

It was the answer Cyril had hoped for but not the one he'd expected. Vale was talking as if it was easy for him to make the decision. "But what about your life there?"

"I don't really have one. I only have two people who matter in my life, and neither of them stays in one place for long. We don't see each other often, and it won't be a problem for them to come and see me here rather than in Boston."

Cyril didn't have to ask to know that one of these people was Russell. He had no idea about the other one, but he suspected he'd find out soon.

"There's also the problem of the Walker family. I know you're already involved, but I don't want you to get hurt because of me." Cyril bit his lower lip. He'd avoided thinking about this until now, but he couldn't anymore. "Maybe it would be better if I left the city. I only have my mother, so it would be easy to move both of us."

Vale squeezed Cyril's hand. "Do you *want* to leave?"

"Of course not. I've lived here all my life, and I've built my business here. I don't want to be pushed out, but I won't put anyone in danger because I'm too stubborn to do the right thing."

"I'll fix this for you."

Cyril wanted him to, but he cared about Vale too much. "Not if it means getting yourself in trouble."

"My line of work means I'm often in trouble, but I know what I'm doing. Besides, we can ask Russell for help. He's still hanging around, waiting to see what happens."

Cyril was aware of that. Russell had taken to texting him every so often. Apparently Russell's friends didn't appreciate his memes, even though Cyril found them quite funny. He'd started sending some of his own to Russell, who was always enthusiastic when he received them. He'd probably get a kick out of meeting Oscar now that Cyril thought about it.

"I'll take care of the Walker family and ensure you won't ever have to leave this place," Vale said, a promise in his voice. "I'll do it to keep you safe but also because it's time for me to be happy. I'll retire, and you can boss me around or do whatever you want."

Cyril suspected that Vale would be bored within a week of being retired, but that didn't mean he couldn't find something else to do. With how things were shaping out to be, Cyril might need a permanent bodyguard, and he couldn't think of anyone better to protect him than Vale.

Vale was almost too perfect. If Cyril had tried to dream up the perfect man, that man would have been close to Vale. Cyril was relieved he wouldn't have to give up his man and happy that Vale seemed to want him as much as he wanted Vale.

Cyril turned and hooked his arms around Vale's neck. "I don't want you to get hurt or make promises you can't keep." But he could already see the tight set of Vale's jaw and his stubbornness in the way he looked at him. Whatever Cyril said, Vale was going to do this, and Cyril could only sit back and watch.

"I'll keep you safe even if you don't want me," Vale promised.

Cyril was already shaking his head. "I thought we'd already gone over that. I do want you."

And since it looked like Vale still didn't quite believe Cyril, he set out to show him. Words might not be enough, but Vale might believe Cyril's actions.

He kissed Vale again. He smiled when Vale's arms went around him, holding him close in a way no one ever had. Cyril felt safe in Vale's embrace, and he couldn't see that changing. He didn't know what would happen with the Walker family, but Vale would do whatever he could to keep him safe, and that wasn't something anyone but Cyril's mother would ever do. It wasn't the main reason Cyril wanted to be with Vale, but it was one of them.

To Cyril, it was important that he felt safe. It was the only way he could relax with someone, and with Vale, he had that. Vale had never looked at him with anything but curiosity and affection. Cyril trusted him not to be afraid of him and to keep him safe. He wasn't sure what he gave Vale in exchange, but whatever it was, Vale seemed to be pleased with him.

Vale made a soft sound at the back of his throat and suddenly got up. Cyril screeched and clung to his boyfriend — he still couldn't believe Vale was his boyfriend — but it didn't last long. Vale turned and leaned toward the couch, gently dropping Cyril to it. Cyril let go, even though he didn't want to, but he didn't want to appear clingy.

Vale didn't hesitate to come back to Cyril's arms, though. Cyril opened his legs to accommodate Vale between them, and Vale plastered their bodies together.

Cyril wanted to be safe, and he'd never felt so safe. He'd

also never felt as wanted as he did with Vale. Every time Vale touched him, like when he pushed up Cyril's t-shirt and pushed down his shorts, told Cyril that he was cherished. It might be too soon to feel that way, but Cyril didn't care. He couldn't stop his heart from galloping forward when Vale was such a perfect man.

He reached for Vale's jeans and quickly undid them. He didn't want Vale to get up, so when Vale tried, he clung to him. He just needed Vale's dick to be out, and he could do that by pushing Vale's jeans down his thighs.

Vale chuckled, the sound turning into a moan when Cyril bit his neck. He wasn't sure what Vale liked in bed — or, as it was, on the couch — and he was eager to find out. It seemed like biting would definitely be on the list.

Vale caught Cyril's lips with his and kissed him almost desperately. It was as if he couldn't get enough of Cyril, which was good because Cyril felt the same way about him. His shorts were halfway down his legs, and they were easier to get rid of than Vale's jeans, so Cyril wiggled until he could get one leg free. Once he did, he wrapped both legs around Vale's waist, his shorts still hanging from one of his calves.

They were both hard, and when their cocks touched, Cyril hissed in pleasure. He could feel the damp head of Vale's cock and wondered how it would taste. He also wondered how it would feel inside him, and if Vale would be inclined to switch things up every so often, but even if he wasn't, Cyril didn't care. He'd take a lifetime of being fucked if that was what Vale wanted.

But right now, both of them seemed to be on board with continuing what they were already doing. Vale rutted against Cyril, and Cyril thrust up, tightening his legs around Vale's waist every time he did so. It was messy, especially with the July heat making them sweat, and Cyril already felt sticky. Maybe they could shower together later.

The friction was driving him nuts, as was Vale's heavy weight on top of him. When Vale gently bit Cyril's lower lip, Cyril knew he was done for. He cried out, prayed no one could hear him, and came.

For a few seconds, he had no idea what was happening around him. Vale was panting against Cyril's lips, and Cyril kissed him because he wanted to and because he could. He felt Vale shudder, and their stomachs became even slicker. The sensation made Cyril wrinkle his nose, but he didn't regret anything they'd just done.

They both stayed where they were, panting until Vale turned his head and yelped. He scrambled off Cyril's body, almost braining himself on a corner of the coffee table when he fell. Oscar was sitting on the table, watching them.

"This is where I draw the line," Vale said as he quickly pulled his jeans up. "I refuse to have him watch us while we have sex."

"What about the rest of the time?" Vale had to know that Cyril would never abandon Oscar, so he'd have to accept both of them if he wanted to be with Cyril.

Vale groaned. "He can stay around the rest of the time, just not when we're being intimate."

If Cyril was honest, he wasn't quite comfortable with Oscar watching them in this kind of situation either, so it wouldn't be a problem. "I'll lock him up somewhere next time."

It didn't matter. Vale had accepted him for who he was, and he'd accepted Oscar, even though he was still uncomfortable with him. That was all Cyril needed.

Now, he just had to make sure the Walker family didn't ruin all of this for him.

CHAPTER ELEVEN

Vale had had enough of waiting. He was used to it in his job, but this was his private life—his *boyfriend*—and he wanted Cyril to feel safe again. That wouldn't happen until the Walker family stopped coming after him, but Vale wasn't sure how to make that happen.

He rubbed the top of Oscar's head as he thought. The easiest way to ensure the Walker family didn't continue coming after Cyril would be to get rid of them, but Vale was only one man. Besides, he wasn't sure it would be worth it. How many people would he have to kill to keep Cyril safe? What would Cyril think of him if he did that?

No, getting rid of the entire family was out of the question. What did that leave? Vale could kill the new head of the Walker family. James Walker's son was the one giving the orders now, so he clearly had to be the one who wanted his father to be reanimated. Vale didn't know much about the family, but he doubted that whoever came after Paul Walker would want the same thing. James Walker only had one son, and once he was gone, the family would go to some cousin or whoever was strong enough to take over and keep the family in check.

Vale didn't care who the family went to. He only cared about keeping Cyril safe, and if that meant killing the entire family, he'd do it. He still hoped to be able to avoid that solution, which was why Russell was coming over. They'd get Rachel on a conference call so the four of them could discuss what the next steps should be.

"Do I need to prepare something else?" Cyril asked as he stared down at the coffee table.

It was laden with food. Cyril and Russell had met at the library, and while Vale hadn't asked about their budding friendship, he knew they were getting close. Cyril had been smiling a lot lately, and Vale knew it was in part thanks to Russell. Russell didn't care that Cyril was a necromancer. He just cared that Cyril sent him funny cat pictures.

But this was important to Cyril, which was why he'd prepared all this food. It would have been too much for Vale, but Russell could eat his way through a grocery store, so he'd be happy to see all of this.

Vale gently put Oscar on the couch and got to his feet. "It's fine. Russell isn't coming over to eat."

"He's coming over to help me, but it doesn't mean I should let him starve." Cyril chewed on his bottom lip and looked down at the table again. "I still have time to go to the grocery store and buy a few more things."

He moved, possibly to do just that, but Vale caught him around the waist and pulled him close. Cyril squeaked but relaxed as soon as he was pressed against Vale's chest.

"Russell is coming here to help you, and with all this food, he definitely won't starve. If he's still hungry after he eats everything, he can go to the grocery store himself or get a burger or something. You don't have to worry about him."

Cyril looked down at Vale's chest. "I want him to like me."

The pain in his voice broke Vale's heart. The only thing Cyril had ever wanted was to be loved. He wanted friends, people who would be there for him, but he'd never had that because people were stupid. What did it matter that Cyril was a necromancer? Why were people so scared of him?

Vale cupped the back of Cyril's head and kissed him. "He already likes you. Hell, I think he likes you more than me, and I've known him for years. You don't have to worry about

Russell, babe. If he wants something or if there's something he doesn't like, he's always vocal about it. Besides, he'll probably be too distracted by Oscar to worry about food."

That brought a smile back to Cyril's lips. "Really?"

"He's going to love Oscar."

"As much as *you* love Oscar?"

Vale snorted. "I'm getting used to him, but I have to admit I still find him a little freaky. Russell will love him at first sight, though."

"I told him I have a pet, but I was afraid he wouldn't take it well if I explained about Oscar. Most people don't. I'm surprised you've accepted him, actually. I expected you to tell me I had to choose between the two of you."

Dammit. Why was Cyril tearing out Vale's heart and stomping all over it? Vale hated every single person who'd be mean to Cyril, even though he'd never met them. If he did, he'd make sure to tell them what he thought of them and their behavior.

"I would never do that," he murmured as he kissed Cyril's cheek. "Oscar is your friend, and I could never even *think* about asking you to give him up. He's a little weird, but I can deal with that."

Vale *was* dealing with it. He wasn't sure he'd ever be able to say he loved Oscar, but he was getting used to seeing the little thing around the apartment. He hadn't even screamed when he'd woken up the other night to find Oscar staring at him from the nightstand.

A knock on the door meant that Vale needed to let go of Cyril, but he wasn't happy about it. He kissed him one last time, then went to the door.

He was careful as he opened, just in case, but Russell's face beamed at him from the hallway. Vale opened the door wider and noticed that Russell wasn't alone.

"Rachel?" he asked.

She grinned at him and opened her arms. "Surprise."

Vale grabbed her and hauled her into his arms. She laughed as she hugged him as hard as he was hugging her. It had been too damn long since they'd last seen each other.

"What are you doing here?" Vale asked as he dragged both her and Russell inside the apartment. "I didn't expect you to come here. Weren't you on the other side of the country?"

"I had to come and meet your boyfriend," she teased as she looked around.

Cyril was still standing by the coffee table, looking like he might bolt at any moment. His nervousness was cute, but Vale wanted him to feel comfortable around his friends.

"There's my bestie," Russell said as he made a beeline for Cyril.

Cyril blinked, but Russell was already pulling him into his arms and patting his back.

"He's a cutie," Rachel murmured.

"Yeah, he is. I don't know how I got so lucky."

Rachel elbowed him in the stomach. "Stop that. You got so lucky because you deserve it. Now you just have to be careful and not fuck it up."

Vale laughed. "I can't make promises."

"Don't I know it," she muttered as she moved closer to Cyril.

He looked bewildered by Russell's excitement at seeing him. Clearly, he didn't understand the kind of person Russell was, but he would soon. Once Russell latched onto someone, there was no getting rid of him, and he'd definitely latched onto Cyril.

"Rachel said you have a pet," Russell said, looking around. "Where is it? Is it a cat or a dog? It doesn't matter. I'm going to become their best friend."

"His name is Oscar," Cyril explained as he looked at Vale.

Vale nodded to encourage him to be honest. Russell was

going to love this and be insufferable for weeks.

"That's a cute name," Rachel said as she peeked around. Her eyes widened when two tentacles appeared from under the couch.

Vale remembered well what it was like to see Oscar for the first time. He hoped Russell and Rachel wouldn't freak out too badly because he knew how important this was for Cyril.

Cyril leaned down and gently pried Oscar from under the couch. He held him to his chest and looked at Vale's friends. "This is Oscar."

Russell *squealed*. That was the only way to describe the sound that came out of his mouth when he saw Oscar. It startled Cyril, who clung harder to his pet as he watched Russell with wide eyes.

"Oh. My. God." Russell stared at Oscar. "What is he? Is he an octopus?"

"Octopi don't have bones," Rachel said.

She was staring at Oscar, too, and while she didn't look as excited as Russell, she also wasn't running out the door, which Cyril took as a win.

"He's not an octopus, even though he looks like one. I don't know what he is, to be honest," Cyril explained. "He's just something I made one day when I was lonely."

"That's a human skull," Russell said.

He looked excited enough to explode. Cyril hadn't expected this kind of reaction, but it warmed his heart.

He glanced at Vale, who was watching them with a smile on his lips. He should have listened to his boyfriend, who knew his friends better than Cyril. He'd told Cyril they wouldn't care about Oscar and would even like him, and he'd been right.

"Can I touch him?" Russell asked. "Please?"

"You can hold him, if he's okay with that."

Russell squealed again and made grabby hands. Cyril was careful as he handed Oscar over. He kept an eye on his pet, but Russell was cautious. He cradled Oscar against his chest and started stroking his skull right away. When Oscar made a purring sound, Russell looked like he was about to pee himself.

"You kept this from me," he said, turning to Vale. "How could you? If I'd known about Oscar, I would have moved in with you and Cyril."

"And that's why I didn't tell you about him. This apartment is crowded enough without adding you to the mix," Vale said.

Cyril had seen them together at the library, so he knew the bickering was normal for them. He turned to Rachel, unsure what to expect from her. Vale had thought they'd have to call her so she could talk with them, but instead, she'd come here.

Cyril wasn't sure what he'd expected, but it wasn't a beautiful blonde girl. She was probably around Cyril's age, although since she was friends with Russell and Vale, she might be older. She didn't look much older than Cyril, though.

Her hair was long, hanging around her face and framing her blue eyes. A smattering of freckles on her nose and cheeks told Cyril she'd recently spent some time in the sun, and she was wearing a pair of black jeans and a black tank top. She'd had a bag when she'd come in, so big that Cyril wondered if it was a handbag or a travel bag. She'd dumped it next to the couch, and it had made a loud sound when it hit the floor, as if it was heavy.

The tattoos that spread down her shoulders were beautiful and colorful. Cyril wanted to take a closer look, but he didn't want to offend her.

"I'm Rachel," she said as she smiled at Cyril. "Ignore these two. They're always bickering."

"I've only seen them together once, but I could already tell that. Welcome to my apartment, and I'm really sorry you had to travel all the way here because of me."

She shrugged. "I'm happy to be here and to help Vale." She sat on the couch, still focused on Cyril. "Why don't you tell me what happened? Vale already told me, but I'd like to hear it from you."

Russell and Vale grew quiet as Cyril settled in his favorite armchair and explained everything from the beginning. There wasn't much to say, but the three of them focused on his every word. Rachel had taken out her phone and was typing on it, maybe taking notes. Cyril wanted to ask, but he didn't dare.

"We need to focus on Paul Walker," Russell declared. "It's the only way to make him understand that he needs to leave Cyril alone."

"How do we do that?" Vale asked. "Besides, do you really think he's going to take a step back because we ask him to?"

"Maybe if we ask him nicely?"

Vale rolled his eyes. Cyril agreed with him. He doubted that Paul Walker would leave him alone, no matter how nicely he asked.

"I guess I could reanimate his father, although unless they froze the body, it's not going to be a great idea," he offered.

"No," Vale said. "Starting to work for them is the worst thing you can do. Once they have you in their clutches, they won't let go."

"I agree," Rachel said. "They're not the kind of people to allow you to leave once you've given them what they want. Once they see what you can do, they're going to try to get even more out of you. They won't care that you don't like it or that you don't want to work for them."

Cyril had known that, but he couldn't see another way out of this. If he couldn't convince Paul Walker to leave him alone, what choice would he have?

"You're also not leaving town," Vale said. "I know you don't want to, and it's not fair."

"Life is unfair," Cyril murmured. "If it's the only way to get them to leave me alone, I'll go."

Rachel patted Cyril's knee. "Why don't we try something else first? I think that talking to Paul Walker could be a good idea. I'm not sure he knows who he's dealing with beyond Cyril, and it could give him pause. Now that he stepped into his father's shoes, I'm sure he has a lot of things to focus on, and that one little necromancer doesn't really matter."

"Or we could kill him," Vale muttered.

"I suppose we should keep that as a last resort," Russell said. "As much as I'm looking forward to the entire family vanishing from the face of the earth, I'm not sure that who-ever would take Paul Walker's place at the end of it would be better. Maybe we should look into that before killing him."

"But whoever takes his place might be inclined to leave Cyril alone, especially if they know we're the ones who killed Paul," Vale pointed out.

Rachel cleared her throat. It was enough to get everyone's attention, which was surprising.

Vale seemed bent on killing Paul Walker, no matter what anyone else said.

"I'll look into who should take Paul Walker's place if he dies," Rachel said. "Once we have an answer to that question, we can decide whether to kill Paul Walker or try to talk some sense into him. I don't care about him, but I don't want any-thing to unsettle the family even more. It wouldn't be good for the city."

"So we wait?" Vale asked, sounding unhappy.

"I know it's not what you wanted to hear, but I think it would be better to wait than to rush ahead without knowing what we're getting into. Just give me a few days, all right? I might even try to contact someone in the Walker family and see if they're willing to at least talk to us. Even if Paul Walker can't be reasonable, someone else might be, and we need to find that someone."

Cyril hated feeling like he was a bother, and right now, he definitely was one. These people didn't owe him anything, yet they were doing what they could to help him. He didn't understand why, but he suspected Rachel and Russell were doing it for Vale while Vale was doing it for Cyril.

Vale wanted Cyril to be happy. He wanted him to be safe.

And Cyril wanted the same.

CHAPTER TWELVE

"Cyril Moreau," Cyril answered when his phone rang.

There was a moment of hesitation before a woman asked, "Are you a necromancer?"

This was generally how these conversations started, so Cyril wasn't surprised by her question. "I am. What can I do for you?"

"I would like to reanimate my mother. It's not a permanent reanimation. I just want to say goodbye."

The woman sounded remarkably calm. Cyril hoped her mother hadn't died very long ago. Sometimes that happened. Sometimes people died and nobody realized they'd passed away weeks—if not months—before. Those were the worst. Cyril didn't have any problems reanimating recent deaths, and older deaths were easy, too, but the ones in between weren't great. He did it if he had to, but he wasn't fond of them.

"Why don't you tell me more about yourself and your mother?"

There was more hesitation. "When can you come? It's kind of urgent."

"I can come today if you need me to."

"That would be great. My name is Eliza Madison."

Cyril wrote down everything Miss Madison told him. She didn't give him many details, but it was enough. He was glad this wouldn't be a permanent reanimation, because he'd done enough of those recently, and this should be fairly easy.

Except for the telling Vale part.

He wouldn't be happy that Cyril had accepted a job. He'd told him to be careful because of the Walkers, and while Cyril agreed, he didn't want to spend the rest of his life locked up in his apartment. He couldn't afford it, anyway. He needed to earn money, and while he had quite a bit put aside and could survive for a while without working, he didn't want to dip into his savings too much. He'd already been out of the game for several days and had refused a couple of jobs. He was done hiding.

After getting everything he needed from Miss Madison, he hung up. Vale was on the phone in Cyril's bedroom, so Cyril had left him alone, but now, he needed to explain that he was leaving the apartment.

He wasn't looking forward to it.

With a sigh, Cyril heaved himself onto his feet. He had everything he'd need in his car, so he didn't have to waste time preparing for the reanimation. He just needed to put on his shoes and tell Vale that he was going.

The bedroom door was slightly ajar, but Cyril still knocked before pushing it all the way open. Vale turned, a smile on his face, only for it to disappear when he took a good look at Cyril.

"I'll call you back," he told whoever he was on the phone with. He quickly hung up and moved toward Cyril. "Did something happen?"

"No. I just got a call for a job, and I accepted it."

"What? Cyril, we talked about this. You can't accept jobs for now. If you need money, I'm more than happy to give you some."

Cyril shook his head. "I don't need money. I need to work. The Walker family might not get their hands on me if I don't, but I won't be able to survive. I'll lose all my clients."

"I understand, but it's dangerous."

"I know." Cyril stepped closer and put a hand on Vale's

waist. "You told me you didn't want me to leave town, and I agree. I don't want to go. I also can't continue hiding in my apartment, though. I don't want the Walkers to win, which is what's happening."

"They could try to grab you."

At least Vale wasn't yelling. He looked scared for Cyril, which Cyril could understand because he was scared, too. The Walker family had to have frozen James Walker because if they hadn't, reanimating him would be a grim occasion, but it meant they'd continue coming after Cyril until they got what they wanted from him.

But he wasn't lying. He had to be able to leave his apartment, and he couldn't if he continued being afraid. His fear would still be there, but he couldn't allow the Walker family to ruin his life more than they already had.

"I'll be fine. This is a quick job, a woman who needs to talk to her mother."

"I'm coming with you."

Cyril wasn't surprised. He was relieved that Vale wouldn't let him go alone. He would have if he'd had to, but knowing he'd have someone to defend him made him feel better. "Thank you. I just need to go to the bathroom and put my shoes on."

Vale gently kissed Cyril. "I'll be ready when you are."

It didn't take long for them to leave the apartment. Cyril was nervous, and not just because of the Walker family. He couldn't help but wonder what Vale would think as he watched him reanimate someone.

Usually, people didn't want to see it. The thought of Cyril doing it freaked them out, and even when he was reanimating their loved ones, they tended not to look at what was happening. Cyril didn't have a problem with that, but he was a bit worried. Vale had seemed accepting until now, but would that change if he saw what Cyril's job consisted of?

Cyril supposed he was about to find out. He didn't want to lose Vale, but they couldn't be together if Vale wasn't fully accepting of Cyril and his job. This was Cyril's life, and he couldn't imagine getting another one.

"You have everything you need?" Vale asked.

"I do. I have a bag in my car, so I don't have to worry about gathering my stuff. There's not a lot involved, anyway. The power comes from inside of me."

Vale smiled. "All right. We're taking my car."

That was fine with Cyril, but they had to stop to get his bag. He understood why Vale wanted them to take the car he'd rented. If the Walker family was watching Cyril, they would know what car he drove. It was better if they used Vale's.

They stopped by Cyril's car to grab his bag, then Cyril climbed into the passenger seat of Vale's rental. He gave Vale instructions so he'd know where to go, then fell silent as he thought about the job ahead. It was weird, but Miss Madison hadn't given him many details about her mother and how she'd died. Usually, it was one of the first things people told him when they called. They wanted to be sure he could reanimate their loved ones, so they gave him details about the way they'd passed.

It didn't matter. He could reanimate pretty much anyone, even if they'd been shot. Hell, once, he'd reanimated a man who'd had both of his legs cut off in an accident. He'd hesitated a while before doing so, and he'd only agreed because the man's family had wanted to say goodbye. He remembered the way the man had clung to his wife and daughters, and he didn't regret giving them that opportunity. He would have refused to do a permanent renovation in that case, but he hadn't been asked for one.

Unsurprisingly, they were going to a funeral home. Cyril could see how tense his boyfriend was as he parked and got out of the car. He kept looking around as if he expected someone to pop out from behind a bush or a car.

Cyril took Vale's hand and squeezed. "I've been here a few times, so I know the place. Everything will be fine. It's just a job, and it won't last long."

Vale nodded, but Cyril could see he wasn't reassured. He didn't think anything would help Vale relax beyond going back to the apartment.

Cyril didn't mind spending a lot of time in his apartment because he loved it, but sometimes, it was too much even for him. He was glad he had this opportunity to leave the house for a bit, but he could admit he'd feel better once they were back home.

Which meant that the sooner he got to work, the sooner he'd be able to relax.

Vale didn't like any part of this, but he couldn't forbid Cyril from leaving his apartment. He needed to continue working, earn money, and show his clients how much he cared. Vale couldn't begrudge him for that, but he could certainly begrudge the Walker family for making it dangerous.

After Cyril kissed him, Vale followed his boyfriend into the funeral home. It was clear the people here knew him from the way they behaved when he stepped into the building. Two men stood by the front desk, and while one of them took a step back, the other hurried to Cyril's side.

"Mr. Moreau," he said.

Cyril smiled at him. "Good morning. A Miss Madison called me."

"I see. We have her mother here, although she didn't warn me you were coming."

"I apologize. I just got a call and didn't have anything else to do for today, so I thought I would come right away."

"It's not a problem. Mrs. Madison is in room three. You

remember where it is?"

Cyril nodded. "I do." He gestured toward Vale. "This is my partner. He'll be coming with me."

The man was clearly curious when he looked at Vale, but Vale barely gave him any attention. His focus was on Cyril and keeping him safe.

"Of course. He's welcome to go with you," the man said.

Cyril smiled, and when he moved toward a door to the side of the room, Vale nodded at the man and followed.

The hallway was short, with only a few numbered doors. Unsurprisingly, Cyril stopped in front of the one bearing the number three and knocked. It took a moment, but when it opened, Vale tensed.

He didn't recognize the woman. She wore a black dress and black shoes, and her brown hair was pulled away from her face. Her makeup was impeccable, and she appeared surprised when she noticed Vale.

"Miss Madison?" Cyril asked. "I'm Cyril Moreau."

"I didn't know you worked with a partner," she said.

"I don't."

"Don't worry," Vale quickly said. "I'll stay out of the way."

She was still frowning, but she stepped aside to let them in.

She was alone in the room, or rather, alone with her dead mother. An elderly woman was stretched out in a dark wooden coffin, her eyes closed, looking remarkably alive. Vale shivered, but he tried not to show it to Cyril. This was what Cyril dealt with every day, and Vale didn't want him to think he was afraid or disgusted.

He wasn't. Vale dealt with death as much as Cyril did, just in a different way. His targets' deaths were much more violent, and Vale was the one who meted them out. He was sure Cyril preferred his kind of job.

Cyril put his bag down on a nearby table and turned to Miss Madison. "You didn't tell me much on the phone. How long do you need me to reanimate her?"

"Just the time to say goodbye," Miss Madison said quickly. "But I wanted to know if she'd be confused first."

"It can happen sometimes. I'm really sorry if it does in this case. More often than not, people who died are a bit confused when they wake up."

Miss Madison nodded. "I see. Can I ask you to cut it off if she's confused? I don't think I could take having to explain to her who I am. She had dementia toward the end, so I realize it's highly probable that she won't recognize me, but I have to try."

Cyril's expression was soft and gentle. "I understand. Well, the dementia will still be there, but we can certainly try."

"I'll pay you even if she doesn't recognize me."

"That's all right. Just tell me when you're ready, and I'll get to work."

Vale stood by the door, giving Cyril space. He'd never seen a reanimation, and he was curious, but even more than that, he was unwilling to let Cyril out of his sight. There weren't any windows in the room, so the only point of entry was the door, and Vale was guarding it. No one would come in to grab his boyfriend.

Cyril stood on one side of the coffin while Miss Madison stood on the other. Vale winced when Cyril gently grasped the dead woman's wrist. Vale could imagine all too well the sensation of touching her, and it made him shiver. He might kill people for a living, but he didn't usually touch their dead bodies after they'd been dead a while.

Vale had no idea what to expect, but it was relatively simple. Cyril focused for a moment, and the woman's eyes blinked open. She looked around, frowning, and started to sit up, but Miss Madison leaned forward. "Mom?"

The woman jerked back. "Who are you?" she asked, looking from Miss Madison to Cyril.

She was starting to panic. She pulled away from Cyril, and when he looked down and saw she was in a coffin, she opened her mouth, possibly to scream.

Vale could only imagine how hard this was on her daughter. Miss Madison had known her mother had dementia, but it couldn't be easy not to be recognized, even after death.

Miss Madison looked at Cyril and shook her head. Cyril reached for Mrs. Madison again, gently touching her arm. "It's all right," he murmured in a soothing tone. "You can go back to sleep. Everything is all right."

It was as if the life leached out of Mrs. Madison. She lay back into her coffin, then closed her eyes again. She stilled, and Vale understood that she was dead again.

"Thank you for doing this," Miss Madison said.

"I'm really sorry you couldn't say goodbye."

Cyril appeared genuinely distraught. He took his job seriously and wanted to help people, which was one of the reasons Vale was falling for him. He was a good man, and Vale hated that he was in danger.

"You warned me, so I knew what to expect."

Cyril looked at Vale. "I'm going to go wash my hands in the bathroom."

"I'll come with you," Vale said as he opened the door. He glanced into the hallway, but it was empty.

A crash made both of them jump. Vale turned to see that Miss Madison had dropped her purse, and everything had spilled out of it. She was on her knees, quickly grabbing her things and pushing them back into the purse. She was showing more emotion now than she had before, and Vale wondered if she'd reached her breaking point. After seeing her mother like this, it would make sense that she had.

She looked up. "I'm really sorry."

"It's all right. I'm sorry for your loss."

Vale turned, but Cyril was gone. Vale narrowed his eyes

when he saw his boyfriend open a door further down the hall-way. He should have waited for Vale, and Vale would make sure to tell him that as soon as he returned. It would take him a few minutes. Vale suspected that Cyril wanted to gather his thoughts, so he turned and went to help Miss Madison.

The sooner this was over, the sooner he could get Cyril home, and he couldn't wait. He hated the feeling that Cyril was vulnerable and that anything could happen at any moment.

Even though Cyril had done everything he could, he hated the feeling that he'd disappointed Miss Madison. It had to have been hell not to be recognized by her mother, even though she'd expected it. She hadn't had the opportunity to say goodbye to her mother when her mother was alive because of dementia, and she'd probably hoped she'd be able to now. Instead, her mother had failed to recognize her.

Cyril tried not to think too hard about it as he washed his hands in the small sink. He had worked here several times, so he knew where everything was. He'd wanted to wash his hands after touching Mrs. Madison, but he'd also needed a moment to breathe.

It always broke his heart when he couldn't help the people who contacted him. If they were willing to pay his rates, it meant this was truly important to them, and he wanted to give them that. Unfortunately, he hadn't been able to do so this time. He'd have to make sure to tell Miss Madison that she didn't need to pay him. The money didn't matter when she'd been unable to say goodbye to her mother.

After breathing in and out a few times, he dried his hands and opened the bathroom door. Vale would probably want to leave right away, and that was fine with Cyril. He expected Vale to be waiting for him in the hallway, but when he stepped out, he couldn't see his boyfriend anywhere. The door of the room they'd been in earlier was open, though, so Cyril moved toward it.

An arm wrapped around his neck from behind. A hand landed on his mouth, cutting off the scream he'd been about to unleash. Warm breath bathed his ear, making him shudder in horror.

"Don't scream, or something bad will happen to your boyfriend."

Cyril swallowed. He could hear Vale talking to Miss Madison, and from the tone of his voice, he was all right. Cyril desperately wanted to get his attention, but what if this man was right? What if something happened to Vale if he did?

"Good boy," the man said as he dragged Cyril backward.

Cyril's heart raced when he realized what was happening. He knew about the back door and had seen it open a few times, but he'd never used it, and he hadn't thought about it until now. He'd just wanted a few moments by himself and to wash his hands, and now he was being kidnapped.

Vale would never let him live it down. He had come with him to protect him, but because of Cyril's own actions, Cyril was being taken away. He was sure Vale would find him, but what state would he be in when that happened? How long would it take Vale?

Would Cyril ever see his boyfriend again?

Chapter Thirteen

"I don't know how to thank you," Miss Madison said as she clutched her bag against her chest and gripped Vale's wrist with her free hand.

Vale didn't want to be rude, but he needed to get to Cyril, so he gently freed himself. "You don't have to thank me. I didn't do anything."

Miss Madison glanced toward the door. "But you did. I'm sorry, I'm a bit flustered. I probably should sit down."

There was a chair nearby, so Vale guided her toward it. As soon as he was free, he moved toward the door.

"Wait," Miss Madison called out, but Vale didn't stop.

He strode toward the bathroom, knocked on the door, and waited for Cyril to answer.

He never did.

After knocking again, Vale opened the door and swore. It was unlocked, and the bathroom was empty. The sink was still wet, but that was the only sign that Cyril had been there. Vale stepped back into the hallway and looked left and right. There were only two doors without a number on them. One was the bathroom, but he didn't know where the other led. He took out his gun and pushed open the door, waiting for a second before peeking out.

A parking lot.

He stepped out and quickly checked all the vehicles parked there, but he already knew Cyril was gone.

Vale had lost him.

He swore and rushed back inside. He wanted to rage, kick

something, and get answers. It wouldn't be the best way to do this, so he restrained himself. He knew where to start.

The room where Miss Madison had been earlier was empty, so he quickly made his way outside. Only one of the men who'd been at the front desk earlier was there, but Vale ignored him as he rushed out the front door. Miss Madison was rushing toward a red car. When she looked back and saw Vale, she broke into a run.

Vale went after her. He reached her as she unlocked the car door, snatching her keys so she couldn't drive away.

"What are you doing?" she asked.

Vale didn't have any problems killing women. Sometimes they were even more evil than men, and while he didn't know if that applied to Miss Madison — or if that was even her real name — he wouldn't hesitate to get answers out of her.

"Where's Cyril?" he asked.

She shook her head. "In the bathroom."

Vale grabbed her by the arm and slammed her against her car. She squeaked, but Vale hadn't hurt her.

Not yet.

He leaned forward. "Tell me where Cyril is."

She swallowed heavily. "I don't know. I was just told to call him and ask him to come in to reanimate that woman."

"She wasn't your mother."

"No. I just did what I was told. I had to."

Vale let go of her, and she slumped against the car. She was clearly petrified, so he believed that she'd felt forced into doing this.

Dammit. This was all Vale's fault. He should have gone to the bathroom with Cyril and stood guard outside of the door while he did what he had to do. He shouldn't have allowed this woman's sob story to distract him.

But he had. He knew who had Cyril, and he needed to get him back before the Walker family hurt him.

He dropped the woman's car keys to the ground and turned. He had his phone out before he reached his car, and he dialed both Russell's and Rachel's phone numbers, putting them on speaker so he could talk and drive.

"Hey," Russell said when he answered. "How's my favorite human? And I'm not talking about you, Vale."

Vale didn't have the time to joke around. "Cyril was taken."

There was a moment of silence before Russell swore. "What happened?"

"The Walker family?" Rachel asked.

"He was called for a job at a funeral home. I talked to the woman who called him, and it was all fake. They grabbed him while he was in the bathroom."

Vale was thankful neither of them asked him where he was while this was happening. He would have told them, but he wasn't looking forward to admitting he'd been so reckless.

But he had been, and because of him, Cyril would suffer.

No. Vale would ensure that Cyril didn't suffer. He'd get him back before the Walker family could hurt him.

"It's a safe bet that they took him to the Walker mansion," Rachel said. Vale could hear her fingertips on her keyboard as she spoke.

"How do we get there?" Russell asked, his voice fully professional. He was taking this seriously because it *was* serious. Cyril was his friend, and he wanted to help him as much as Vale did.

"I'll send you the coordinates. Security is high, though. I'm going to need some time to hack into the system so they don't see you arrive."

"Do what you have to do," Vale ordered.

"We're going to need a moment to grab your stuff and get there, anyway," Russell said. "I'm already on my way."

Vale didn't have to go back to Cyril's place. When he'd

moved in with him, he'd left all his weapons in the car because he didn't want Cyril to be uncomfortable. He'd only brought his gun up to the apartment, which meant everything else was still in the trunk. He could go straight to the Walker mansion.

Which was precisely what he was planning on doing.

The Walkers would regret taking Cyril.

"Do they know to expect us?" he asked.

"I'm sure they do," Rachel answered. "Both you and Russell defended Cyril from them before, so they'll probably expect you to do so again. Be careful."

"We always are," Russell said.

Vale didn't care about being careful today. He only cared about getting his boyfriend back before Cyril could be hurt. Hopefully that wasn't the first thing the Walker family would do. They needed Cyril to reanimate James Walker, which meant they'd want him in one piece and not in pain. If he refused, though, they wouldn't hesitate to torture him until he agreed to do what they wanted.

Vale wasn't planning on giving them enough time to do so.

"I'll see you there," Russell said.

"Don't be late," Vale ordered before hanging up.

At least after this was over, the Walker family would never bother Cyril again. Vale should have done this on day one, but he hadn't wanted Cyril to be afraid of him or see him for what he truly was.

A killer. Someone who didn't hesitate to take someone's life if he was paid to do so. In this case, he wouldn't even be paid. He'd exterminate the Walker family with pleasure because he wanted to—because they'd dared hurt one of the only three people he cared about.

Cyril was in trouble. He knew who had taken him because it

would be too big of a coincidence if two different people wanted to force him to reanimate someone, but knowing that didn't help. He couldn't fight the Walker family, especially not on his own.

After that man had grabbed him in the hallway at the funeral home, he'd been dragged out through the back door and thrown into the back of a van. They hadn't tied him up, so he'd scrambled to try to get out, only to meet a gun cocked at his face. The man who'd grabbed him had climbed into the back of the van with him, and he'd been keeping an eye on him as the man in front drove them.

Cyril was terrified, but he knew Vale would come for him. It wouldn't take him long to realize what had happened and who had taken Cyril. When he got his hands on whoever had ordered this, Vale was going to have fun with them, and Cyril was tempted to ask if he could watch. He didn't know if his stomach could take it, but he might try anyway.

"So this is what a necromancer looks like?" The man driving said.

Cyril might be so frightened that he wanted to scream, but he didn't want to show it. These two were goons sent by Paul Walker. They wouldn't hurt him, which meant he didn't *have* to be afraid of them. He raised his chin and glared at the man still holding a gun in his direction. The man seemed to find it funny.

"I expected more, too," the man with the gun said. "Maybe someone scarier."

"That body is too old," Cyril snapped.

The man with the gun frowned. "What?"

"Did you freeze him?"

"What are you talking about?"

"If James Walker wasn't frozen, his body will be too decomposed for me to do anything with it. Do you really want to see me reanimate a man who looks like a zombie?"

The man grimaced and glared at Cyril. "Shut up."

Talking to these guys wouldn't help. They weren't in charge, and they wouldn't let him go even if he begged.

He leaned back and swallowed. He'd been called to reanimate decomposed bodies a few times, and it was never fun. It had never been for permanent reanimations. Usually, the police had needed to talk to them, or the bodies had been found a while after they'd died, and the family had needed urgent information. It was as disgusting as one could imagine. Human bodies weren't made to stay the same after they died. That was one of the reasons Cyril was planning to get cremated when he passed away. He didn't want anyone to reanimate him, and he didn't want to become food for worms, even though he understood he'd be dead and wouldn't care by that time.

But James Walker would care. If Cyril reanimated him, he'd get his mind and soul back. He'd be able to see himself, see how degraded his body was. Reanimation was never easy for a dead person to deal with, but finding themselves reanimated into a body they didn't recognize and were horrified by? It would be enough to drive anyone nuts.

Cyril wasn't sure how long they'd been in the van when they finally stopped. He could only look outside through the windshield, but the man with the gun had ensured that he wouldn't peek. It didn't matter, anyway. Cyril was pretty sure there was no way he'd get out of this on his own. The Walker family would have to be much more stupid and reckless than they'd been until now, but he didn't think he'd be that lucky.

No, if he was going to get away, it would be because Vale, Russell, and Rachel would come to get him.

They would. At the very least, Vale would come, but Cyril was sure that Russell would be right there with him. From what he'd gathered, Rachel's job wasn't in the field, but it didn't mean she wasn't working hard on getting him back.

The van doors opened as soon as they stopped, and two more men appeared. They grabbed Cyril by the arms and hauled him out of the van, making him stop in front of the guy with the cigarette from the grocery store parking lot.

Cyril glared at him. He could have lived a happy life without ever seeing this guy again.

The man had a cigarette in hand. He blew the smoke in Cyril's face. "I told you we'd see each other again, Moreau," he drawled.

"I'm not reanimating you when you die of lung cancer," Cyril muttered.

The man gestured at the goons to drag Cyril inside.

Cyril didn't resist, knowing it would be useless, but looked around. If he managed to escape, he wanted to know where to go.

The problem was that the house was massive. More than a house, it was a mansion, with two staircases curling from the foyer to the first floor. There was a round table in the middle of the foyer with a massive green plant on it and a lot of marble. Cyril wasn't sure if the art hanging on the walls was original, but even if it wasn't, it had to be expensive.

He hadn't expected anything different from the Walkers.

Cyril was pushed past the table between the staircases. There was a hallway there, and as he walked, he noticed a kitchen. There was a woman inside, cooking, but she didn't even turn around. She kept her focus on what she was doing. Either she was terrified that she'd be hurt if she didn't, or she didn't care what happened to Cyril.

They stopped in front of a door at the end of the hallway. Cigarette-guy opened it, revealing stairs that went down. He gestured at the goons, and they pulled Cyril forward.

They were in a basement. Cyril had been afraid before, but now he was terrified. He wouldn't be able to escape from the basement if the only way out was the door from which he'd just entered. And how were Vale and Russell going to get in?

A man waited for them at the bottom of the stairs. Cyril had seen pictures of him in the newspapers and on the news, so he recognized Paul Walker. The man looked like he'd aged ten years over the past two months, though. There were dark shadows under his eyes, and his hair was mussed and dirty-looking. He was pale, although that could have been because of the harsh white light in the basement.

Or maybe because of the smell.

Cyril gagged as his gaze stopped on a figure stretched out on a table. They hadn't frozen James Walker. "I can't reanimate him like that."

Paul Walker grabbed Cyril's arm and hauled him forward toward his father. Cyril stumbled, and for a horrifying moment, he thought he'd fall right onto the body. Thankfully, Paul Walker gave him a shake, keeping him on his feet.

"You'll do what I order you to do," he snapped.

Cyril glared at him. "Do you really want your father to come back like this?"

"He'd want to."

"Would *you*? Look at him. I'm not even sure he'll be able to walk if I reanimate him. He definitely won't be able to look at himself in the mirror, and I wouldn't be surprised if he lost bits and pieces every time he moved."

Paul Walker shook him again. "Do what you're here for, necromancer. Reanimate my father permanently."

There was no way Cyril would do that. Maybe he could reanimate him just for an hour or two, but what would happen to him when he died again? He wanted to believe that Vale and Russell would get to him before that happened, but he couldn't be sure. He'd seen the house and the goons standing around. He had no doubt there was a complicated security system and more guards than he could count. Vale might need time to get to Cyril, which meant that Cyril might have to go along with what Paul Walker was asking him to do.

Paul Walker leaned closer. His breath smelled of alcohol and unbrushed teeth. It wasn't as bad as James Walker's smell, but it was enough to make Cyril wrinkle his nose.

"Reanimate him. If you don't, you'll die," Paul Walker ordered.

"Where would that leave you? There's only one other necromancer in the city who can reanimate a body permanently, and I already warned her to leave town."

Paul Walker smiled a grim, terrifying smile. "Maybe I shouldn't kill you, then. Maybe I should kill your mother."

Cyril shuddered. He'd known Walker would threaten that, so he wasn't surprised. He couldn't continue resisting. He would never forgive himself if something happened to his mother, and he had faith in Vale. He'd get him out of here and make Walker pay—both of them if needed.

"Fine," he said, shaking off the man's hand from his arm.

He stepped closer to the body and shuddered. The smell was enough to make him gag again, and he hadn't even touched the body yet.

James Walker's skin wasn't pink anymore. It was a mottled dark green mixed with shades of browns and blacks. It had started slipping, which made touching him complicated, because Cyril didn't want to throw up on him.

Paul Walker gave him a push. Cyril knew that delaying this wouldn't help. He tried to ignore the feeling of the dead skin under his fingertips and the awful, sickly-sweet smell of death. He focused on his power, pushing some of it into the body. Whatever Paul Walker said, Cyril wasn't about to reanimate his father permanently. He just needed a few hours, maybe a few days. He knew Vale and Russell would get to him before James Walker died again and that they'd keep his mother safe if it was necessary.

The body made an awful sucking sound, and Cyril snatched his hand away. Paul Walker started to say something, but his father's eyes opened, cutting him off.

James Walker's eyes were black.

Cyril looked away and tried not to throw up. He'd seen this kind of thing a few times, so he knew what to expect, but that didn't make it any less horrifying. He hated Paul Walker for forcing him to do this. He hated James Walker for being a monster, even before he died.

"Dad?" Paul Walker asked as James Walker pushed himself into a sitting position. One of his fingers lost a bit of skin, which flopped on the cement floor. Cyril's stomach churned.

James Walker turned, swinging his legs off the table. Paul Walker stepped toward him, reaching for him. Cyril didn't understand how the man could want to touch his father in the state he was in.

James Walker opened his mouth, a croak coming out as his blackened tongue slipped between his lips.

His head exploded.

Vale didn't hesitate to put a bullet between James Walker's eyes. The man was already dead, anyway, and being permanently gone would be better than being the fucking zombie Vale had just seen him become.

Vale didn't have the time to consider the horror of what Paul Walker had forced Cyril to do. No matter how much the stench in the basement made him gag, he needed to keep Cyril safe, and with James Walker permanently dead, Vale wouldn't be surprised if his son took it out on Cyril.

"I could have done without the zombie," Russell muttered from next to Vale as he shot one of the goons.

"Shut up before I turn *you* into a zombie," Vale snapped back before shooting another guard.

Once Rachel had taken care of the security system, it had been fairly easy to get into the house. She'd been able to tell them where every single guard was, so they'd neutralized them, tied up the cook and the few maids they'd found hiding, and headed straight for the basement. Rachel had seen Cyril being dragged there on the camera feed, but there were no cameras in the basement itself, so Vale and Russell had gone in not knowing what they'd find.

Vale shot in the direction of Paul Walker, but the man jumped behind the table where his dead father was still spread out. Cyril just stood there, looking horrified and pale, and Vale prayed it was because of what he'd been forced to do and not because he was finally seeing Vale in his natural habitat.

The habitat of a professional killer.

"Grab Cyril," Russell said. "I'll take care of the minions."

Vale nodded and moved toward his boyfriend. Cyril appeared to be in shock. He kept looking from James Walker's dead body to Vale, but he wasn't moving. Vale didn't want to spook him or scare him more than he already was, so he put his gun away when he reached him. It was a stupid thing to do, but he trusted Russell to have his back.

"Cyril? Babe?" he called out.

Cyril blinked at him. "I'm not going to be able to reanimate him again," he croaked. "There's no head left. I mean, I could try, but he'd be a headless corpse. He wouldn't be the man he was before."

Vale carefully reached for Cyril. He didn't jerk away when Vale touched him, so Vale dragged him into his arms and wrapped himself around him. Cyril sucked in a breath and hooked his arms around Vale's waist, clinging on as if he was afraid Vale would disappear if he didn't.

"You're going to regret this," Paul Walker snarled as he appeared from behind the table.

Vale's gun was in his hand and aimed at Paul Walker in seconds. The man stared down at it as if considering whether or not to push Vale. He probably thought Vale wouldn't shoot him, but he'd be wrong.

"Twitch a muscle in my boyfriend's direction, and you'll join your father," Vale threatened.

"I'll make you pay for this," Walker threatened, but he stayed where he was behind the table.

He kept glancing at his father, and even though Vale didn't care about any of these people, he couldn't imagine what was running through Walker's mind. He'd been convinced his father would come back, but there was no way that would happen now.

"You can try," Vale told him. "But if you as much as touch a hair on Cyril's head, I'll make *you* pay for it. As long as you leave us alone, we'll do the same with you and your family." Even though someone really ought to kick their asses. That was the police's job, though, not Vale's.

Walker snarled and leaned forward. "You took my father from me, and it's not something I'll forget. You might have won this fight, but I'll come after you with everything me and the family have."

"Enough!" a man shouted.

Vale arched a brow in the direction of the man who'd spoken. He recognized the guy from the parking lot. He wasn't smoking now, which was kind of a pity because Vale would've taken the smell of cigarette over the smell of decomposing body.

He'd looked into the guy after their encounter in the parking lot. The man's name was George Miller, and he'd been James Walker's second in command for years. Vale suspected George should have taken over after James had died, but the Walker family had been led from father to son for decades. James Walker's father had been in charge before him and his grandfather before then.

"You don't give me orders," Paul Walker snarled.

"I do when you're behaving like an idiot," Miller snapped. "This is over. I told you that reanimating your father was a bad idea, but you ignored me. You used the family's resources to go after the necromancer when it was obvious it wasn't a good idea. I've had enough of this, and since your father is permanently gone now, this is over. You need to stop."

"I always knew you were smarter than the guys in charge," Russell said. His gun was aimed at Miller, but his body language was fairly relaxed, giving Vale hope.

Only Walker and Miller were still standing. Russell hadn't killed all the goons, but he'd wounded them, and it would take them some time to recuperate—if they ever did. There would probably be more coming, which meant Vale needed to get Cyril out of the house, but this had to be over first. He didn't want Cyril to have to look over his shoulder for the rest of his life.

Miller stared at Russell for a moment before nodding. "You won't get any more trouble from us," he said. "We won't bother the necromancer, either. This is over."

Walker tried to get to Miller, but Miller raised his gun. Walker froze, staring at him as if he'd betrayed him. Vale supposed he had. He didn't know what would happen or who would take charge, but he didn't care. This was none of his business. Only Cyril was, and he was almost safe.

Vale looked at Russell, who nodded. That meant he had everything in hand, so Vale put away his gun and focused on Cyril again.

He guided his boyfriend toward the stairs. "Come on, babe. Let's go home."

"It's over?" Cyril asked.

"It is. You heard the man. The Walker family will leave you alone from now on."

A sob escaped Cyril's lips, and he pressed a hand against it. He allowed Vale to guide him up the stairs, then through the house toward the backyard. Vale wouldn't make him climb the wall like he and Russell had, but he'd noticed a back gate, so they wouldn't have trouble reaching the cars.

They were stepping out of the kitchen door when a shot rang through the house. Cyril jumped and pressed harder against Vale, and while Vale was curious and slightly afraid for Russell, he knew Russell could take care of himself. Vale's complete focus had to be on Cyril, so he didn't stop moving until they reached the cars.

"Is Russell okay?" Cyril asked as Vale settled him into the passenger seat.

"I'm sure he is. He'll meet us at your apartment, so you'll be able to see for yourself soon enough."

Cyril nodded and leaned back into the seat. Vale looked at the house one last time, grinning at the sight of Russell stepping out the kitchen door. The asshole had stopped to make himself a sandwich. He was chewing enthusiastically, and when he looked up and saw Vale staring, he waved at him with the gun he was holding in his other hand.

Vale rolled his eyes. He shouldn't have worried. Russell always made it out of these situations in one piece.

So had Cyril. It was over, and Cyril was safe.

Vale was never letting him out of his sight again.

Cyril was safe. He had a hard time believing it, and every so often, he touched his chest to reassure himself that he was still breathing.

For one terrifying moment, he'd thought he'd die. When he'd seen James Walker's head explode, he'd known he wouldn't be able to fix that. He'd expected Paul Walker to take it out on him, and the man would have, but Vale had been there. He'd saved Cyril. He'd come for him when Cyril thought it was over, and Cyril could never thank him enough for that.

He opened his mouth to say something, but Vale reached over and squeezed his knee. "You don't have to thank me. I should have been more careful at the funeral home, but I let that Madison woman draw me in with her sob story."

Cyril frowned. "What do you mean?"

Vale sighed. "That woman wasn't her mother. She asked you to come to the funeral home because she wanted to give the Walker goons the opportunity to take you. When I realized you were gone, I went after her, and she admitted it."

Cyril closed his eyes. He hadn't expected that, but maybe he should have. He wasn't surprised that the Walker family had tried everything to get him to reanimate James Walker.

Well, it looked like the only one who wanted that was Paul Walker. The guy with the cigarette had taken a stance and allowed Cyril to leave, and Cyril hoped that meant that the Walker family wouldn't come after him in the future. He wouldn't put it past them, even though cigarette-guy had said they wouldn't, but for the moment, he wasn't afraid.

The Walker family had come after him, and he'd made it out alive. He wasn't even hurt. Vale had found him and was taking him home, and if Cyril played his cards right, he'd have Vale by his side for the rest of their lives. Vale would continue protecting him, seeing things Cyril didn't even notice and ensuring that no one hurt him.

"I want you to stay with me," Cyril blurted out. "I want you to move into my apartment. I know you have to go back to pack up your stuff, but I don't want you to find a new place here. I don't want you away from me."

Vale glanced away from the road to smile at Cyril. "That's a relief because it's what I was planning. I don't think I can let you out of my sight after what happened today."

Cyril slumped against the seat. He could rest even more easily now that he was sure Vale would stay with him.

He watched the city outside the window, feeling better by the time they reached his apartment. His legs felt like jelly, but he managed to climb out of the car just as Russell parked next to them. He grinned at Cyril and rushed out of the car, wrapping his arms around him and hauling him off his feet.

"I'm glad to see you're all right," he said, squeezing Cyril so hard he squeaked.

"All thanks to you."

"Well, Vale helped."

Vale grumbled as he gently guided Cyril out of Russell's arms and toward the door. "I helped, he says," he mumbled. "As if I didn't do most of the work."

"I worked hard, too," Russell said as he rushed forward to enter first.

Cyril recognized that behavior now. Russell wanted him and Vale to wait outside while he checked the inside of the apartment. The Walker family might not be a danger anymore, but both he and Vale would want to be sure, and Cyril couldn't begrudge them that. It would be a relief to know that no one was waiting in his apartment, hiding behind a door.

Russell vanished into the apartment and reappeared a few minutes later, holding Oscar. Oscar's tentacles were waving around, and he looked slightly agitated, but he calmed down right away when Cyril took him. He climbed up Cyril's shoulder, settling there with his tentacles wrapped around Cyril's neck.

Vale stared at Cyril before shaking his head. Cyril didn't have to ask to know what he was thinking, but that was all right. He didn't need Vale to understand why he cared so much about Oscar.

"The apartment is safe," Russell said. "I talked to Miller after he shot Walker because Walker tried to attack him, and he promised he's going to keep an eye on the guy. He didn't explain much, but from what I gathered, the man went off the rails after his father died. Instead of taking his father's place at the head of the family, he became obsessed with the thought of reanimating his father. When Cyril told him no, he freaked out. He kept his father's body in the basement and continued sending men after Cyril."

"He could have at least frozen his father," Vale muttered.

Russell shuddered dramatically. "Yeah, that was horrifying." He looked at Cyril. "I can't even imagine how you felt, having to reanimate him."

"It's not the first time I've had to do something like that, but I don't do it regularly, and I don't plan on changing that."

"No zombies for you," Russell said with a nod. To Cyril's surprise, he pulled him into his arms and kissed his cheek. "Don't get into more trouble before I can move to the city, all right?"

"You're moving?"

"Yeah. I feel it's time for me to put down roots, and since Vale is going to be here with you, I decided it would be a good idea to join you guys. Besides, Oscar's here."

The day had been horrifying, but Cyril couldn't stop himself from smiling. He wasn't just gaining a boyfriend. Something told him that if he continued spending time with Russell, the two of them would become fast friends. He couldn't wait.

"Well, I might need a permanent bodyguard, but I promise I'll try to stay out of trouble," he said.

"You already have a permanent bodyguard," Vale declared. "I'm moving in with you, aren't I?"

"It doesn't mean you have to follow me around all the time. I'm sure you'll find something better to do with your days."

Vale shook his head. "Who better to do it than me? I'm sure we can find a way to work together."

Cyril wasn't sure they could. After all, he and Vale had met because he kept reanimating Vale's targets and annoying him. Their jobs were as different as they could be.

But Vale was retiring. He wouldn't be killing people for a living anymore, so maybe they *could* work things out.

Either way, Cyril couldn't wait to try.

Epilogue

Cyril's apartment was full of people and noise. Normally, he wouldn't have enjoyed it, but today, he found himself unable to stop smiling.

He could hear his mother in the kitchen, cooking up a storm, looking happier than she had in a long time. When Cyril had told her that Vale was moving in with him, he'd expected her to ask him if he was sure and maybe tell him they should wait until they knew each other better. She didn't know what had happened with the Walker family, and Cyril hoped it would stay that way. He had no intention of explaining to her that he'd been kidnapped and forced to reanimate a decomposing body. Besides, that was all in the past now. He was safe, and Vale would make sure nothing like that ever happened to him again.

But Cyril's mom hadn't tried to stop him and Vale from moving in together. When Cyril had told her, she'd hugged both of them and had winked at Cyril. She seemed to adore Vale, and the feeling was mutual. Vale had told Cyril that he didn't have a family beyond Russell and Rachel, and he'd taken to Cyril's mother like they'd always known each other.

Cyril loved it. He'd only ever had his mother and Oscar, but he'd made a place for Vale effortlessly, and now, he couldn't imagine his life without his boyfriend. It wasn't only that Vale kept him safe. Mostly, Vale was there to love him and cherish him, which was what Cyril had yearned for all these years.

The fact that Vale came with two best friends was a plus.

Cyril loved both Russell and Rachel, although he hadn't gotten to know Rachel as well as Russell. She'd left town only a few days after the mess with the Walker family had happened, and she had yet to return. Russell, on the other hand, was still here. He and Vale had gone to Boston for a few days to get Vale's things packed up, but they were back, and as of now, they were almost done getting all of Vale's stuff into Cyril's apartment. It would be a tight fit, and Cyril hadn't lived with anyone since he'd left his mother's house, but they'd make it work.

He heard Russell laugh just outside the front door. Then Vale grumbled something in answer. Cyril could never have imagined having a professional assassin as a boyfriend, but he wouldn't have it any other way. Vale had promised that he was retiring, and so far, he hadn't gone out on any jobs. Cyril had told him he didn't want him to feel forced into anything, but he didn't think Vale did. He'd wanted to leave that life behind even before meeting Cyril, and he seemed to be settling in easily.

Cyril hoped he was. He didn't want Vale to regret being with him.

Hopefully, the Walker family would stay out of their lives. Cyril hadn't heard anything about them so far, not even on the news. They'd almost vanished, and while he was sure they were still in the city with their hands in many crime pies, it wasn't his problem, and he hoped it never would be. His job was to reanimate dead people. He wanted nothing to do with crime or crime families.

An arm wrapped around his shoulders, making him jump. Vale looked worried, but Cyril quickly leaned against him and kissed his jaw.

"I didn't mean to startle you," Vale said as he nuzzled Cyril's ear.

Suddenly, Cyril wished his mother and Russell would

leave. The thought made him smile because even though he wanted to be alone with Vale, he'd have plenty of time to do so later. He and Vale lived together now.

"It's fine. I was just thinking."

"About what? Are you already regretting letting me move in with you?"

"Never."

Vale's body relaxed. Sometimes, Cyril had to remember that he wasn't the only one who didn't know what to do in a relationship. This was as new to Vale as it was to him, and they were learning it together.

"Good because I'm not going anywhere," Vale said as he pressed a kiss to Cyril's hair. "We're done bringing up the boxes. Russell is insisting on staying for dinner, but I can kick him out if you want."

Cyril shook his head. "He can stay. My mom's cooked enough for an army, and Russell and I have been planning his pet."

Vale groaned. "Do you really have to make him one of those things?"

Cyril didn't, but Russell was enamored with Oscar and had asked Cyril if he could have a similar pet. Cyril didn't see the harm in that. He didn't think Russell was ready to retire just yet, even though he was moving close to them. If he wanted a pet, he'd need something that could survive even if he left it alone for a few days, maybe even longer. Cyril would be happy to take in whatever pet he created for Russell if Russell had to work, but this was such a small thing to do for Russell when Russell had saved his life. Besides, it would give Oscar a playmate, and Cyril was excited about that.

He was excited about a lot of things now that he had so many people in his life. Having a boyfriend and a few friends might not be a lot for most people, but for Cyril, it was every-thing. He'd gone from only having his mother to feeling like he was part of a family, and he wanted to make Vale, Russell, and Rachel happy. If Russell wanted a skeleton pet, Cyril would make him one.

Russell barged into the room, looking around. "Where's my favorite little skull?"

Oscar rushed out of the bedroom as soon as he heard Russell's voice. Watching them, Cyril was convinced more than ever that creating Russell a pet was a good idea.

It was hard to believe that Cyril would have none of this if he hadn't been called to reanimate two of Vale's targets. He didn't know what had happened to the two men after he'd done his job, but it didn't matter to him.

He had everything he could ever have asked for and everything he hadn't dared to allow himself to dream of.

ABOUT THE AUTHOR

Catherine is the creator of several series, most of them paranormal, including the Whitedell Pride Series and the Gillham Pack Series. While she graduated in translation, she decided to go the writer's way because it was more fun to create her own stories and characters.

She's been living in Italy for more than twenty years, but she's a daughter of the North—Belgium to be precise—and she misses it so much that she's already planning to move back.

She loves pizza—probably too much —her son, her pets, and of course, books. She sneaks some reading time into her schedule every time she has five minutes free from writing, demands from her various pets and son, and lastly, housework.

Connect with her:

lievens.catherine@gmail.com
BookBub:
https://www.bookbub.com/authors/catherine-lievens
Website: https://authorcatherinelievens.com/
Facebook: https://www.facebook.com/catherine.lievens.9
Facebook Group:
https://www.facebook.com/groups/411788002341528/
Twitter: https://twitter.com/authorCLievens
Newsletter: http://eepurl.com/c-uvKn

.